PINS, PAINS AND PROMISES

SOME STORIES ARE STITCHED IN SILENCE, SCARRED BY PAIN AND SAVED BY THE PROMISES WE REFUSE TO BREAK.

Dr. Manisha T. Kundnani

AF517381

BlueRose ONE .com
Stories Matter
NewDelhi • London

BLUEROSE PUBLISHERS
India | U.K.

Copyright © Dr. Manisha T. Kundnani 2025

All rights reserved by author. No part of this publication may be reproduced, stored in a retrieval system or transmitted in any form or by any means, electronic, mechanical, photocopying, recording or otherwise, without the prior permission of the author. Although every precaution has been taken to verify the accuracy of the information contained herein, the publisher assume no responsibility for any errors or omissions. No liability is assumed for damages that may result from the use of information contained within.

BlueRose Publishers takes no responsibility for any damages, losses, or liabilities that may arise from the use or misuse of the information, products, or services provided in this publication.

For permissions requests or inquiries regarding this publication, please contact:

BLUEROSE PUBLISHERS
www.BlueRoseONE.com
info@bluerosepublishers.com
+91 8882 898 898
+4407342408967

ISBN: 978-93-7139-786-5

Cover design: Daksh
Typesetting: Tanya Raj Upadhyay

First Edition: July 2025

Dedication

To every woman who's carried a silent ache,

To every couple chasing a heartbeat,

and to every promise made in the quiet,

You are seen...

You are remembered.

Table of Contents

Chapter – 1
Silence Speaks More Than Words

The rhythmic ticking of the big analog clock on the wall made Tanvi more anxious with each passing minute. Each measured click felt like a tiny hammer against her frayed nerves. It was an unwelcome reminder of how long they had been waiting.

Though the clock hung directly in front of her, she checked the time on her phone again.

11:21 AM.

Their appointment had been scheduled for 10:45.

She muttered under her breath, "It's 11:21."

Tarun's eyes, fixed on his laptop screen, fingers moving in a steady, practiced rhythm. He seemed detached, though she knew better. Detachment was just another form of coping. The delay didn't seem to bother him outwardly, but Tanvi knew the quiet storm beneath his calm surface – she'd seen it too many times.

Her words, soft though they were, finally pulled his attention. He glanced up.

Their eyes met, and in that brief collision of gazes, years of shared hope, weariness, and unspoken sorrow swelled between them like a tidal wave no one ever dared to acknowledge aloud.

He gave her a small, almost imperceptible nod – a silent *'I know'* – then quickly returned to his screen, his fingers resuming their steady, mechanical typing.

Tanvi shifted in her seat, tucking a loose strand of hair behind her ear.

She was striking in an understated way – the kind of beauty that didn't scream for attention but lingered in the memory. Soft, kohl-lined eyes framed by long lashes, shoulder-length hair that she usually wore in effortless waves.

Today, she had thrown on a peach kurta with delicate vines of silver thread embroidery along the sleeves and paired it with ivory palazzos – a look she could pull off with the ease of someone who lived and breathed fabric and design. It was one of her own designs, from the boutique.

Tanvi was a fashion designer and owned a small boutique, a labour of love she had built from scratch, crafting delicate traditional and fusion wear for women who wanted elegance without pretence. However, she wondered if anyone ever noticed such details in a place like this.

Beside her, Tarun was her opposite, in both appearance and temperament. Tall, lean, with neatly cropped hair and wire-rimmed glasses that made him look a little more serious than he really was. He was dressed in a simple blue shirt and well-fitted pants, his black MacBook open on his lap – always connected, always working.

An IT professional working in finance, Tarun's world was one of numbers, risk assessments, and tight deadlines. While Tanvi saw the world in textures and colours, Tarun saw it in algorithms and probabilities. And yet, for thirteen years, they had managed to stitch their contrasting worlds together, though lately, the seams were beginning to feel a little frayed.

The waiting room, designed to be comforting, only seemed to amplify the disquiet within her.

Pale blue walls bathed in a soft, natural light. A neat stack of well-thumbed magazines no one touched. A large Ganpati idol perched in a corner next to the reception, it's serene smile offering just a little amount of solace.

On one side, a wall labelled "The Fertility Wall' bore framed photographs of grinning couples holding infants swaddled in pink and blue, alongside hopeful quotes in delicate cursive. "*Miracles take time.*" "*Faith makes things possible.*" "*Hope never disappoints.*" And many more.

The irony was suffocating.

A row of cushioned chairs lined the space, occupied by other couples avoiding each other's gaze, their faces etched with the same mixture of hope, fatigue, and quiet desperation.

The television mounted in one corner played muted Bollywood songs no one was watching. The only sound punctuating the heavy silence was the relentless tick-tock of that damn clock, interspersed by the faint ringing of the reception phone.

Tanvi shifted in her seat, crossing and uncrossing her legs. Her mind was caught in a turbulence of what-ifs and worst-case scenarios. No amount of warm paint and plush chairs could have hushed the cacophony echoing in her head.

Across from her sat another couple. The woman's rounded belly was visible even beneath the loose folds of her pale-yellow kurta. Tanvi's eyes locked onto her belly and stayed there. And automatically her hand drifted to her own belly – flat, empty, still waiting.

No matter how many times she pasted a brave face, there was a hollow ache inside which no one could see.

How many mornings had she crouched in the bathroom, clutching a white plastic stick with a single pink line glaring back at her?

Negative.

Again.

And again.

Each month, a fresh wound would layer over the old ones until she no longer knew where one heartbreak ended and another began.

She had lost count of the syringes she'd lined up on the bathroom counter – 'those tiny pins and pains', promising maybe this time. How many times she'd clutched her phone in the middle of the night, googling pregnancy symptoms, diets, success stories, miracle tips from strangers in anonymous forums- but all in vain!

The woman in the yellow kurta caught her staring and offered a soft, understanding smile. It was kind, meant to be reassuring. A silent '*you will be a mother too someday*'. But, kindness sometimes hurts more than cruelty does. Tanvi forced a polite half-smile in return, but it felt brittle, like a glass about to crack.

A nurse passed by carrying a tray of tiny cups filled with steaming tea. The faint aroma filled the whole waiting room area. Tarun reached out and took a cup, murmuring a polite thank you. He held the cup in his palm, letting the warmth seep into his hands without taking a sip. Tanvi noticed the way his thumb tapped the edge of the cup, as he continued staring onto his laptop screen.

Even the drive to the clinic had been heavy with silence. The usual traffic, the chatter of Radio Mirchi jockeys, Bollywood songs cycling through nostalgia and heartbreak, filled the spaces where conversation should have been. Tanvi had tried to think of something light, something normal. A comment about the new cafe opening near their apartment. A complaint about the ridiculous potholes. But in her mind, there was only a carousel of questions and longing.

A young nurse in dark blue scrubs appeared in the hallway, holding a clipboard and some forms.

"Mr. and Mrs. Tarun Mehra?" She called softly.

Tarun raised his hand in acknowledgment. The nurse came closer, offered a tight smile, and handed them the writing pad with a ballpoint pen.

"Could you please fill in your details? The doctor will call you in shortly."

Tanvi took the form.

Patient Record – it read.

The script was familiar - too familiar, she knew it a bit too well now. Name. Age. Address. Married for how many years. Previous treatments. Any pregnancies in the past, etc etc.

That last question always landed like a slap.

Pregnancies in the past:

NONE.

It was what she wrote every time. But it wasn't the truth.

They say you should never lie to your doctors or your lawyers. But here she was, scribbling a lie, slowly, in careful capital letters. Lying about the one thing she'd once had. The one thing she was now desperate for.

How could she write the truth?

This was the one chapter of her life she had never confessed to Tarun in their thirteen years of marriage.

It was a long time ago. A short-lived affair. Raghav Chaddha. Yeah, she remembered the name well. 'Old fires leave the deepest scars', and this one was difficult to forget for various reasons. She hadn't spoken his name in over a decade, yet here it was, uncoiling in her mind like a snake disturbed from hibernation.

She remembered so little of him now – the sharp cut of his jaw, the rough stubble, the dimpled grin. The way he made her feel invincible, careless, and reckless. The pregnancy had been just a blur of fear and secrecy, ending before it even had a chance to be anything more. She hadn't wanted it then. She couldn't have had.

Though she had shared everything with Tarun, this was one thing she just couldn't share with him. She was scared – scared of being judged! The truth clung to her like second skin – impossible to shed, yet invisible to the world, more so now when she was struggling to get pregnant.

In a society like theirs, where a woman's worth was still, in many ways, measured by her chastity, by her ability to uphold family honour, an unplanned pregnancy before marriage was more than a personal mistake. It was a scandal. It was a shame. It was the kind of whispered sin that could stain a family name, that could ruin marriage prospects, turn relatives into strangers, and reduce a young girl's life to hushed conversations behind closed doors.

Tanvi had often imagined what it would have been like to confess this to Tarun before their wedding. Would he have understood? Or would he have recoiled – not from the act, but from the crushing weight of what society would say? How would she have faced her parents, her future in-laws? The same people who now prayed daily for her womb to fill, blissfully unaware it once was. The thought alone brought a chill to her spine.

Some truths, she'd decided long ago, were safer buried. Not because she didn't trust Tarun, but because she didn't trust the world they lived in.

And now, as life cruelly circled back, she wondered if it was some sort of cosmic punishment. A debt come due.

A voice tugged her back.

"Mr. and Mrs. Mehra? Please come with me."

It was the same nurse.

Tanvi's heart lurched. She stood too quickly, feeling a flash of dizziness. Tarun gently folded his Mac, carefully placing it back in its black sleeve. He got up and gently placed a hand on Tanvi's back, steadying her.

"Ready?" He asked softly.

She nodded, though the word felt hollow.

They followed the nurse down a softly lit corridor. The walls were lined with watercolours of blooming flowers – peonies, lilies, marigolds. Symbols of life and new beginnings.

The irony wasn't lost on her. This was a place people came to when those very things had betrayed them.

As they reached the doctor's room, Tarun squeezed her hand gently. It was a warm, familiar touch, and for a fleeting moment, it anchored her. No matter how distant they sometimes felt, here, now, they were still walking through this storm together.

The nurse opened the door, and the muffled world of the waiting room fell away. The tick-tock of the wall clock, the faint ring of the reception phone, the smell of tea. Tanvi realized, life went on here. Between heartbeats and hope, between verdicts and second chances, life quietly marched on.

She took a deep breath and stepped inside.

Whatever waited on the other side, they would face it, together.

Chapter – 2
The Name That Shouldn't Be

The consulting room was nothing like Tanvi had imagined.

Soft ivory walls, a tall window letting in strips of gentle sunlight, and shelves lined with books and potted succulents. It smelled faintly of lavender and something clinical beneath it – a mixture Tanvi had grown familiar with over the years.

A small Ganpati idol rested on the doctor's desk, and besides it, a photo frame with the words "*Miracles Happen Here*". A bouquet of fresh lilies rested on the corner table. It had a Big card saying - "Thank you Dr Meera, thank you for making our dreams come true."

For a moment, it almost felt peaceful. Almost.

Her gaze quickly moved to the side wall. It had medical charts pinned on the walls - images of embryos, hormone cycles, fertilised eggs at different stages – she knew all this by heart now.

The woman sitting behind the large white desk wasn't what Tanvi expected either.

Dr Meera Shah.

A name they'd heard through whispered recommendations, anonymous online forums, and hopeful friends of friends. She was said to be kind, patient, and someone who took as much care of a patient's heart as she did of their medical records.

She didn't look like any of the doctors Tanvi had met in the past – the ones with stiff white coats, clipped words, and eyes that either pitied or patronised. She looked different.

There was something unhurried about her presence.

She was a petite woman in her early forties, dressed in a soft blue linen saree, the colour matching to the wall colour at the reception. Soft waves of dark hair with few gold streaks brushed her shoulders, and a small red bindi sat perfectly centred on her forehead. Her eyes – warm, brown, kind – carried the steady calm of someone who had seen enough heartbreak to know the importance of hope.

There was something almost angelic about her.

"Good morning," Dr Meera greeted, her voice gentle yet certain.

"I apologize for the wait. Weekends can be a bit unpredictable here."

"It's alright," Tarun replied, while Tanvi managed a polite nod, though her pulse drummed louder than the clock on the wall.

The doctor gestured for them to sit. She opened a thick folder resting beside her tablet, flipping through old records, blood test reports, prescription slips, and case notes from clinics where Tanvi had taken treatment in the past.

Tanvi watched the doctor's brows draw together for a moment as she skimmed a particular page – the details of their second failed IVF attempt – before smoothing out again. She took a long time to go through each paper, each investigation in detail. This silence was more frustrating than the silence in the waiting room.

"I've gone through your file," Dr Meera said, finally looking up, her eyes meeting Tanvi's. "It's been a long, difficult journey for you both."

God, if only you knew, Tanvi thought, her chest tightening.

She gave a faint, mechanical nod.

"I can see how hard you've fought. The follicular monitoring, IUI cycles, the IVF attempts... the chemical pregnancy last year. It must have been devastating."

Tarun cleared his throat, a small, sharp sound. His hand reached over to touch Tanvi's wrist.

Dr Meera continued, her tone thoughtful but kind. "I think it's time we take a slightly different route. I'm recommending IVF again – but this time with Preimplantation Genetic Testing. PGT helps us screen embryos for chromosomal issues before transfer. It won't remove all risks, but it will improve your chances significantly."

Tanvi exhaled a breath she hadn't realized she was holding.

"How... how much improvement?" She asked quietly.

"Well, while nothing is ever guaranteed in fertility treatments, with PGT, we can select the healthiest embryos for transfer, reducing the risk of chromosomal abnormalities and increasing implantation chances." She leaned forward slightly. "I won't sugar-coat it – it's a demanding process, physically and emotionally. But it's doable. And you're still young, Tanvi. That works in your favour."

Tanvi nodded, though a part of her wanted to scream. How many times had she heard you're still young? And yet every cycle, every month, felt like another grain slipping through the hourglass.

"What does PGT involve exactly?" Tarun asked.

Dr Meera smiled, appreciative of his directness. "A standard IVF cycle – ovarian stimulation, egg retrieval, fertilization, embryo culture, and genetic testing before choosing which embryos to transfer. Only embryos found to be genetically normal would be transferred.

But before we begin, we'll need updated baseline investigations. Hormonal panels for Tanvi, infection screenings, AMH, and a couple of other markers. And Tarun – we'll need a fresh semen analysis here, including DNA Fragmentation Index this time."

Tarun's expression remained neutral, but Tanvi saw the stiffening of his jaw. She knew he hated these parts of the process. The endless tests. The silent, cold lab rooms. The quiet implication that maybe he was the problem too.

"Who would be handling the... procedure?" Tarun asked, his tone practical, business-like.

Dr Meera flipped through her tablet. "I'll be taking care of your case along with our senior embryologist, Dr. Raghav, who will handle the embryo culture, PGT and transfer process."

The room tilted.

For a second, Tanvi was sure she'd misheard.

Raghav.

The name lodged itself in her throat like a shard of glass. Her vision blurred at the edges, a rush of memories she'd spent years locking away breaking through like a flood.

"Is everything alright, Mrs. Mehra?" Dr Meera's voice brought her back.

Tanvi managed a tight smile. "Yes... yes. Just... it's a lot to take in."

Dr Meera nodded, offering her a reassuring glance. "I understand. I'll explain the entire protocol, and we can decide if you'd like to start in the next cycle or take some time."

As the doctor outlined hormone injections, follicular scans, and retrieval procedures, Tanvi's mind wasn't in the room. It was back in a cramped college canteen, on a monsoon-soaked evening, with a boy whose laughter used to feel like home.

Tarun reached for her hand again, squeezing it gently. It was a rare tenderness these days. She clung to it like a lifeline, blinking away the sting in her eyes.

"I'll have the nurse schedule your baseline tests and bloodwork," Dr Meera concluded. "And if you have any questions – any doubts – please don't hesitate to reach out."

She jotted some notes into their file and pressed the button next to her desk. It was a calling bell. The same nurse who escorted them to the room reappeared.

"Please assist them with blood tests and other investigations", Dr Meera instructed the nurse, closing the file gently, unaware of the storm she had inadvertently unleashed.

"Thank you," Tarun said.

Tanvi forced another nod.

As they left the room, her pulse was like a drumbeat in her ears. The world slowed. The name hung in the air like a struck note, sharp and out of place.

"Raghav"

Tanvi's stomach flipped. Did I hear that right? She glanced at Tarun, but he seemed oblivious, calm.

It can't be. No... Did she really say that? Or am I hallucinating?

Her thoughts spiralled wildly.

Even if she did, there must be hundreds of Raghavs. Thousands may be. And even if it's – he wasn't a doctor. He was into something else... biotechnology, wasn't it? Or IT? Or was it biomedical engineering? That was years ago. And this is Mumbai, not Delhi.

Tarun hadn't reacted. He was scrolling through his phone, arranging something on his calendar, completely unfamiliar to the storm surging inside her.

Tanvi's mind was racing. Images she thought she had long buried surfaced back- crooked smile, old bike, cutting chai and late night Maggi.

She tried to keep her face impassive, but her heart was hammering against her ribs.

The name looped in her head.

Raghav, Raghav, Raghav.

Was it fate? A coincidence? Or life's cruel sense of humour?? Was it some kind of cosmic punishment?

Was she hallucinating? Imagining connections where none existed?

She tried to steady herself with logic.

It's a common name. It's just a name.

But deep down, in that old part of her heart she tried so hard to bury, she knew **some old ghosts never stay buried.**

Chapter – 3
The Boutique Blues

They scheduled the tests for the following week. Tarun had meetings, some unavoidable, and as much as both of them wanted to get it over with, life, like always, had other plans.

The car ride back was quiet at first, the steady hum of the AC filling the silence between them. Tanvi stared out of the window, watching the chaos on the streets – the honking autos, metro constructions, and billboards. One of the billboards said-

"SEX"-

now that you have our attention, eat at Subway!"

Tanvi couldn't help but laugh.

Her smiling face caught Tarun's attention. What made you smile?

"Nothing", she said. "Can we stop for a quick subway, I feel famished."

"Sure", Tarun replied and turned the car to a narrow lane. He knew the place well. Tanvi's boutique was just in the next lane. He pulled the car to one side of the road and stopped.

"What will you have?" Tarun asked.

"My regular", Tanvi said. "And can you get me a diet coke?"

"Sure", Tarun said and got off the car.

Tanvi was alone in the car for that moment. Her favourite song was playing on FM- "*Kahin door jab din dhal jaaye, Saanjh ki dulhan badan churaaye...*" Tanvi started humming along and for that instant, she forgot all her stress, the treatment, Raghav and everything else. She was peaceful, momentarily.

Tarun returned with two wrapped spicy Italian footlongs, a Diet Coke and a cappuccino.

"Here you go", he passed one wrap and Diet Coke to Tanvi.

"Thank you. I was starving."

"I think the doctor sounded positive", Tarun said while munching on his wrap. "This PGT thing... it sounds safer. And maybe... maybe it's our chance."

Tanvi managed a small nod. "Yeah... IVF with genetic testing. She seemed hopeful."

"Better than false hopes", Tarun muttered, finishing his wrap.

The discussion made Tanvi restless again. The peace was gone. Her mind again started spiralling around clinic and Raghav, the name that shouldn't be.

But none of them actually mentioned the name. Maybe Tarun hadn't even noticed it, or maybe it was so insignificant to him that it hadn't registered. But for Tanvi, it was a name that hadn't belonged in that room. It had no business resurfacing in this chapter of her life.

The rest of the ride to the boutique was again quiet.

Tarun gave a gentle peck on Tanvi's cheek before she got off the car. "Don't worry, we will figure this out, you have a great day ahead. See you in evening." His words felt reassuring.

"Yes, we will, you too have a great day", said Tanvi and got off.

The Boutique

Her boutique was a small, cosy space tucked away in a quieter lane near the main market.

"Lace & Love" - the hoarding outside read. The shopfront was simple – a glass window displaying a tastefully draped lehenga and an indigo hand-embroidered kurta set, both designed by Tanvi herself.

The brass bell above the glass door chimed as Tanvi pushed it open. A waft of sandalwood-scented air greeted her. Inside, racks of pastel organza sarees, delicate *chikankari* kurtas, and shimmering fusion gowns lined the walls. The scent of sandalwood incense mingling with the warm fragrance of freshly steamed fabric filled the place.

Bolts of fabric lay unfurled across the central table – deep maroons, shimmering ivories, and vibrant peacock blues. Bridal season was in full swing.

Tanvi loved this place. It was her sanctuary, the one thing she had built from scratch – a space where her creativity could breathe.

Anisha, her young assistant, looked up from the billing counter.

"Good morning, ma'am."

Tanvi forced a smile. "Morning, Ani."

She set her bag down and flipped through the appointment book. Marriage season meant back-to-back clients, anxious mothers and brides-to-be fussing over blouse cuts and sequin shades.

Three bridal trials, two new clients, and a final delivery scheduled for the afternoon- read the appointment diary. The day promised to be relentless.

Good.

Work, she'd learned, was the only thing that made the emptiness bearable. A full schedule left no room for wandering thoughts, for pangs of jealousy, for lingering memories.

Or at least it used to.

As she arranged a set of silver-threaded dupattas, her mind involuntarily drifted back to the clinic. To Dr Meera's gentle voice. And to that name.

"Raghav."

She hadn't seen him in last fifteen years, but just the sound of his name was perturbing. She could still picture the curve of his smile, the teasing glint in his eyes, the way he'd held her hand during rain-drenched college afternoons. And then – the pain. The betrayal. The endless nights alone after it ended.

A sudden sharp voice pulled her back.

"Ma'am? The Malhotra bride is here for her fitting", Anisha called from the front.

Tanvi composed herself, smoothing her hair before stepping into the trial room area.

The bride, a tall girl with dusky skin and kind eyes, beamed as Tanvi entered.

"Ma'am, your designs are magic. I can't believe this is mine."

Tanvi smiled, warmth radiating through her for the first time that morning. "You'll look beautiful, Aanya. Let's see how it fits."

As she adjusted the dupatta over the girl's shoulder, Tanvi felt a sudden jab in her heart. Aanya was barely twenty-six, talking vivaciously about her honeymoon plans and her dream of starting a family "as soon as possible." There it was again – that sting, sharp and familiar. She'd grown used to it, like a lingering old wound that occasionally flared up, but it still left her anguished.

Between appointments, Tanvi ducked into her office – a small room lined with swatches and sketches, and framed photos from past brides. She sketched a few new designs, her hand moving automatically, while her mind played an entirely different reel – of a name spoken softly in the clinic, of a face she hadn't allowed herself to remember in years.

The bell chimed again, signalling another client. Work called. Life moved on.

By late afternoon, the boutique was still buzzing with customers, her assistants rushing around with fabric swatches and iced teas. Fittings, last-minute alterations, and consultations about dupatta drapes and zardozi borders.

Yet grief was stubborn. It waits, like an uninvited guest in the corners of our mind. It came now, in the form of a message.

Her phone vibrated on the table beside her sketchbook. "Meghna's Baby Shower - Sunday 4 PM. Hope to see you. Can't wait to celebrate with all our girls!"

Meghna was Tanvi's BFF from school days.

The message was in the form of a video reel, A cheerful illustration of a stork carrying a bundled baby. 'Join us for a Baby Shower in honour of Meghna & her little one!'

Her throat tightened. She should feel happy for Meghna. She was happy for Meghna. But a crushing ache settled in her chest. How many baby showers had she attended in the past years? And how many carefully worded excuses had she made to avoid them? Another gathering of glowing women with round bellies and beaming husbands, and she an outsider pretending to smile. Another milestone that belonged to everyone, but her.

She stared at the date – next Sunday. Just days before their IVF cycle would begin.

Tanvi put the phone face-down and took a deep breath. A customer called her name. She turned, slipped on her practiced boutique-owner smile, and walked over, the grief folding itself away – not gone, just tucked out of sight.

But somewhere behind her measured steps and cheerful consultations, Raghav's name still echoed in her mind. What a cruel coincidence! It can't be him, she told herself again. He wasn't a doctor. He was doing some technology thing back then.

And yet... the name stayed.

By evening, the boutique began to empty. The last of the clients had left with promises to WhatsApp reference pictures, and her assistants were folding dupattas, restacking boxes, and locking the cash drawer. The marriage season rush, though exhausting, had always been a distraction Tanvi relied on. But today, her mind hadn't stayed still for even a minute.

She stood by the glass window as the sun dipped low, streaking the sky in shades of orange and lavender. The street outside was quieter now, a lone tea vendor packing up his stall, cars weaving through traffic, the occasional whiff of roasted peanuts from a passing hawker.

She looked down at her phone again, her fingers hovering over the message notification from Meghna. There was no escaping it. Baby showers. Birth announcements. Happy family holiday photos. They arrived like relentless waves – each one like a new stone, weighing her down with grief.

With an aching heart, she finally replied to the message - "Can't wait to be there. Looking forward. Loads of love. Tanvi."

She said bye to Anisha and stepped out into the evening air. The ache in her lower back reminded her how long the day had been. She hailed an auto. As the auto rickshaw rattled through Mumbai's evening traffic, her mind wandered – back to the doctor's room, to the calm, gentle-faced woman with kohl-rimmed eyes and a soothing voice.

"Our senior embryologist Dr Raghav will assist with the case", the doctor had said.

And there it was again – that name, that shouldn't be. Her stomach twisted.

It can't be him.

But what if it was? What were the odds? Raghav was in biotech back in college – working on some dissertation about stem cells, she remembered vaguely. He was never going to be a doctor. He hated clinics, hospitals, anything remotely clinical.

But people change, don't they? It had been over fifteen years. Who knew what turns life had taken for him?

Tanvi considered asking Tarun when she reached home. Something casual. What was that doctor's full name again? Dr Raghav what? But the thought of bringing up even the name in their home made her uneasy. What if it wasn't him? What if it was? And worse, what if Tarun sensed something in her voice, a tremor of a memory she had no right to carry into this part of their life?

The auto slowed as it turned onto her street. Tanvi realized she'd been holding her breath.

Let it go, she told herself. It's just a name.

But deep down she knew - **Names had a way of returning when you least wanted them to. And this one, clearly wasn't done with her yet.**

Chapter – 4
The Ghost of Yesterday

The name wouldn't leave her mind.

Tanvi lay in bed that night, staring at the ceiling fan as it lazily spun above her. Tarun slept beside her, his breathing soft and even, a comforting rhythm she usually found soothing. But not tonight. Not with the past clawing its way back to the surface.

Raghav.

It had been fifteen years since she'd last heard that name spoken aloud. And just like that, the carefully locked room in her memory burst open, flooding her with images, voices, and scents she had buried deep.

It was a pleasant February evening when she first met him.

She remembered the exact moment –

Delhi 2010

The music was too loud, the room too crowded, and the cheap vodka too warm – but none of that mattered to Tanvi. It was Mahi's birthday, and the tiny apartment off Kamla Nagar was bursting with students, laughter, and the kind of restless energy that came with being twenty and feeling invincible.

Tanvi stood in a corner, dressed in a blue kurta and ripped jeans, sipping from a mismatched plastic cup, pretending to enjoy the party. She wasn't much of a drinker, and she hated the chaos of these gatherings – the lights, the sticky floors, the constant hum of half-drunken conversations. But Mahi was her best friend, and skipping her birthday wasn't an option.

"You look like someone just told you your cat died", a voice said beside her.

Tanvi turned, startled.

A tall, lean guy with unkempt hair and laughing eyes stood there, holding a cup of his own. The checked shirt, blue jeans, and the faint aroma of his perfume – there was a certain rough-edged charm about him, not conventionally handsome, but magnetic.

"Excuse me?" She raised an eyebrow.

He shrugged. "I'm just saying – you're at a party, and you look like you're mentally solving math problems."

"I don't even like math", she replied.

"Good. Me neither. I'm Raghav, by the way."

She shook his hand, the warmth of his palm catching her off guard.

"Tanvi."

"Well, Tanvi, since you hate being here as much as I do, how about we get out of this room before the music gives us both permanent hearing loss?"

She hesitated, glancing around. She barely knew him. But something about his easy confidence and the glint in his eyes, made her nod.

They slipped onto the tiny balcony, the cool night air a relief against the heat of the apartment. Delhi's chaos was quieter here, the occasional honk drifting up from the street below, and the upbeat track of '*Aahun Aahun*' from the party playing in the background.

"So," Raghav said, leaning against the railing. "What's your excuse?"

"For what?"

"For hiding at parties."

She laughed, for real this time. "I don't know. I'm just... not good at these things. Too many people pretending to like each other."

He nodded as if he understood completely. "Yeah. It's exhausting. But the balcony people are the best kind. The ones who escape."

Tanvi laughed again.

Tanvi found herself drawn in. He was nothing like the boys she knew – blunt, funny, and alarmingly honest. There was no pretence with Raghav. He laughed too loudly, didn't care what people thought, and had a reckless streak that made her heart race.

They talked for hours. About college, about how she dreamed of opening her own boutique one day. Raghav was doing Engineering, final year. Biotechnology."

By the end of the night, when he offered to walk her back to her hostel, she said yes without hesitation.

They strolled through empty lanes, streetlights bathing the road in amber. And when he paused, halfway to her hostel, and brushed a stray strand of hair from her face, something inside her shifted.

"You have beautiful eyes, Tanvi", he murmured, and kissed her.

It was clumsy, unexpected, and perfect in the way first kisses often are.

And just like that, a chapter began.

But neither of them in that beautiful moment imagined how short-lived some beginnings could be.

Within weeks, they were inseparable – as if an invisible thread tugged between them, pulling them closer.

Late-night walks around campus.

Endless cups of cutting chai at Sharma's canteen.

Secret rides on his battered Pulsar, hair whipping against the wind.

Conversations that stretched from Bollywood classics to aliens and existential dread.

He made her laugh in a way no one else did. Made her feel seen in a way she hadn't even realized she had craved.

And then, somewhere between the teasing and midnight calls, things turned physical.

She remembered the first time like a dream.

His hands were trembling slightly as they fumbled with her dupatta, her heartbeat loud enough to drown out the world. It wasn't planned. It wasn't perfect. But in that moment, it had felt like the most natural thing in the world.

They promised it was casual.

It wasn't.

Within months, jealousy, possessiveness, and whispered fights crept in. The high of forbidden romance gave way to the fear of being caught, of futures that didn't align.

And then came the storm she hadn't seen coming-

A missed period!

A hastily bought pregnancy kit!

Two trembling pink lines!

Tanvi could still remember the way the bathroom walls closed in around her, her knees buckling as she stared at the result. Fear, shame, disbelief – it all came crashing down in one suffocating wave.

Her breath coming in jagged gasps that fogged the mirror. The reflection showed a stranger, pupils blown wide with terror, lips trembling around a scream she couldn't voice.

When she told Raghav, his face had gone pale.

He paced the room, running his hands through his hair, muttering things she couldn't decipher.

"This... this can't happen, Tanvi. You know this, right?" He'd said, his voice cracking.

She had hoped for something different.

They fought.

Fought like they never had before. Words were hurled. Accusations, fears, disappointments – all laid bare.

Within days, Raghav made arrangements.

A discreet clinic, a rushed procedure, hushed instructions.

It was over in less than an hour. But the aftermath stretched for years.

She walked out of that clinic clutching a crumpled prescription slip and an ache she never quite managed to lose. They tried to pretend things were normal, but it was like trying to build a house over a burial ground. Eventually, it crumbled.

By the time final year exams arrived, Raghav was gone. He left without a proper goodbye – a brief, awkward text that read "Take care, Tanvi."

She buried the memory deep. Never spoke of it again. Never told anyone. Never told Tarun, even though he knew everything else about her.

Some truths were too sharp to touch.

Now, fifteen years later, that ghost was circling again.

Was it the same Raghav? Could life be so twisted as to throw them into the same room again, all these years later with Tarun by her side and the irony of infertility hanging over her head?

Tanvi closed her eyes, trying to sleep.

But all she could see was the glint of the dark, mischievous eyes – **The Ghost of her Past.**

Chapter – 5
The Whispered Shadows

Though the waiting room looked the same, it just felt different. Tanvi couldn't say why – maybe it was the haze of anxiety clinging to her skin.

A fresh set of hopeful, exhausted couples sat clutching folders and filling forms, eyes flickering towards the clock every few minutes. The same Ganpati idol watched over them. The TV today was playing "*Hey Ram Hey Ram*" dhun. She otherwise loved listening to this mantra and it brought her a lot of solace, but not today. Her mind was too restless since her last visit to the clinic. Everything just felt heavier this time.

Tarun was filling out his consent forms while Tanvi sat unusually still, her palms clammy against the leather of her handbag. She couldn't explain it, but every time someone in scrubs passed, her breath caught. The rustle of a lab coat, the soft tread of Crocs on polished tiles – each one made her spine stiffen.

You're imagining things, she told herself. Paranoia.

After filling the consent forms, Tarun started fiddling with his phone, occasionally scrolling through emails, occasionally, watching the sports update on mute. His knee bobbed in restless rhythm, betraying his nerves even though he barely spoke.

A nurse called out, "Mr. Tarun Mehra, for sample collection, please."

Tarun stood, offered Tanvi a tight smile as he squeezed her hand.

"Back in a bit."

Tanvi nodded, forcing a smile she didn't feel.

The nurse handed Tarun a small plastic container covered in a polythene covering and directed him to the collection room.

As the door to the sample collection room closed behind him, Tanvi exhaled. She was alone now. She shifted in her seat, pretending to browse a year-old magazine abandoned on the side table. The other couples around her wore the same mix of hope and exhaustion – young women scrolling through their phones, men looking everywhere but at the walls covered with fertility success stories.

And then – it came.

A low, warm chuckle. Faint, yet clear. A voice. She couldn't make out the words, only the sound. It came from across the corridor, from the hallway leading to the lab area. rising above the muffled conversations of nurses and receptionists.

Tanvi's heart gave a sudden, traitorous leap.

It wasn't possible. But she knew that laugh.

She'd once heard it on rain-soaked college afternoons, sitting under an umbrella at the canteen, legs brushing, hearts foolishly entangled.

She turned toward the sound. Her body reacted before reason could intervene. She stood up, craning to glimpse something.

A tall figure in pale blue scrubs. She caught only the side profile. Sharp jawline, dishevelled hair. The same familiar gait – quick, efficient, impatient. The tilt of the head. The way his hand moved mid-sentence.

Her heart flipped in her chest.

A junior nurse trailing behind called out softly, "Raghav sir, These reports..."

The words hung in the air like a sudden gust.

Her breath caught.

"Tanvi?" A gentle voice which startled her.

It was the receptionist calling her name for her blood test.

Tanvi tore her gaze away.

“Coming”, she said, her voice unsteady.

But her pulse wouldn’t settle.

The phlebotomy room was a tiny, over-lit chamber smelling of alcohol swabs. The nurse chatted about the traffic, the relentless heat, etc etc. Tanvi barely registered the sting of the needle. Her mind kept straying. To a voice, she wasn’t supposed to recognise. To a face, she hadn’t seen in over a decade and a half.

By the time she returned to the waiting area, Tarun was back, tapping a message on his phone.

“All done?” He asked.

She nodded.

“Another week for the reports and baseline scans”, Tarun said. “Then we begin.” He tried to sound upbeat.

Tanvi’s thoughts, however, were still down that corridor.

“Did you... happen to see a doctor while you were in there?” She asked, trying to sound as casual as she could manage to.

Tarun shook his head. “Just a nurse. Why?”

“Nothing, Just like that.” She forced a smile.

He glanced at her, puzzled for a second, then shrugged. "Hungry?"

"A little."

They left.

On the drive home, Tarun chatted about the office work, weekend plans, and how the traffic was lighter than usual for a Thursday. Tanvi nodded wherever required or replied in monosyllables. But inside, she was still in that corridor.

Once they reached home, she excused herself, saying she was tired and retreated to the bedroom.

The warm glow of bedroom lamps did nothing to ease the cold knots inside her.

That evening, back home, Tanvi lay on the bed with her phone. The ceiling fan spun lazy circles overhead. Tarun was on the couch, half-watching a cricket match, half-typing on his laptop.

Tanvi scrolled through Instagram. Food reels. A bride flaunting her *mehendi*. A new designer's boutique launch. A motivational quote.

And then – a familiar name in the 'Stories' tab.

Dr Aditi Varma. An old acquaintance from her college years. Now a gynaecologist at a well-known hospital. Curious, Tanvi tapped the story.

A video reel from an IVF conference.

A crowd shot. Doctors mingling, posing, someone giving a talk at the podium. A banner in the background: Advances in Embryology and IVF techniques, 2025, Mumbai.

The camera panned over a group of people. And there almost at the edge of the frame. Tall, familiar smile. The same sharp jawline, though a little older, a little more seasoned. A slight crinkle around his eyes when he smiled. The same unmistakable warmth in his face.

It's Him.

Tanvi's stomach lurched. Her throat went dry.

She stared, as if willing herself to be wrong.

The story played on, a shot of wine glasses clinking, people laughing, oblivious to the quiet storm it had stirred in one silent viewer.

She checked the people tagged in the story, and there it was, in bold white text, along with many other names at the bottom of the screen: @drraghavchaddha.

Tanvi let the phone drop to the bed. Her heart pounded so loud she thought Tarun might hear it.

Fifteen years of silence. And now, in the one place she'd hoped to leave the past behind, here he was. Not a figment of memory, not some coincidence. Not some other man with the same name.

An embryologist. The irony made her chest ache.

She considered deleting Instagram. Throwing the phone against the wall.

Instead, she turned off the screen, lay back, and stared at the ceiling fan spinning its endless loops.

The room was quiet, except for the soft murmur of cricket commentary.

It can't be him, she told herself again.

But it was.

What now?

Should she tell Tarun? Pretend it was nothing? Would she even be able to look Raghav in the eye if their paths crossed at the clinic? Or worse – what if he recognized her first?

Her heart raced. A dull ache pressed against her ribs, old wounds tugged open by the weight of a name.

Outside the window, the city carried on as if nothing had shifted. A child's laughter echoed from a neighbouring balcony. The shrill whistle of a pressure cooker sounded from a kitchen nearby.

But inside Tanvi's world, everything had changed.

And she wasn't ready.

And something in the pit of her stomach told her – *this was only the beginning.*

Chapter – 6
Sleepless Scrolls

The apartment was silent. Just the occasional hum of the refrigerator and the soft purr of the AC. Tarun had fallen asleep long ago, his soft, steady breathing rising and falling beside her. But Tanvi lay awake, her eyes fixed on the phone screen glowing against the dark.

She knew she shouldn't.

She knew better.

But curiosity had its own way of turning into obsession.

Her thumb hovered over the Instagram search bar. Raghav Chaddha.

She hesitated. Her rational mind screamed at her to stop.

What are you doing, Tanvi? What possible good could come out of this?

But her heart – that foolish, reckless thing – had already won.

The search bar auto-filled before she even finished typing.

There he was.

@drraghavchaddha

Profile picture: a simple black-and-white photo of him standing in front of some lab equipment, arms crossed, and that same quiet confidence on his face.

She clicked.

The grid loaded slowly in the dim light of their bedroom.

Mostly work-related posts – conference photos, embryology lab shots, ovum pickup procedures (tastefully obscured, of course), articles on PGT, and awareness campaigns for infertility treatments.

No selfies. No family pictures. No wedding photos. Not a single frame that showed a wife. Or a child. Or even a girlfriend.

His bio read:

Clinical Embryologist. IVF & ART Specialist. Making babies every day.

Dreamer. Hope-giver.

Tanvi stared at the words.

Hope-giver.

She scoffed softly. Funny, considering how much hope he'd taken from her once.

She scrolled further – snaps from some award ceremony in Delhi, a reposted article featuring him in an IVF journal, a video from a fertility awareness drive.

Nothing personal.

Nothing she was looking for. She wasn't even sure what she was looking for. And why?

Did she want to see him married and settled? To know if he was a father? Or did she secretly want him to be alone, like some strange, unspoken punishment issued by the universe on her behalf?

The rational voice in her head fought to surface.

Why do you even care, Tanvi? It's been fifteen years. You're married. You have a life. A husband who loves you. You're about to start a family. Why poke at wounds that almost healed?

But her heart argued back.

Because some people aren't just people. They're pieces of you.

And Raghav had been that. A piece of her youth. A piece of her recklessness. A piece of who she might have been if life had taken a different turn.

She spent the next hour scrolling through his tagged photos, which were few and mostly professional. A couple of group shots at conferences. A blurry picture from a cricket match, but even that gave away nothing.

No mentions; no comments from a "wifey" or a partner; no birthdays celebrated in cosy cafes; no vacation pictures by the beach; just work; embryos; conferences; labs – a sterile, meticulously curated life.

Maybe that's what it meant to be a hope-giver now.

By 3:45 AM, her eyes stung. Her mind ached. She tossed the phone aside, burying her face into the pillow, silently cursing herself.

She felt pathetic.

Old wounds should stay sealed. She should be better than this.

But grief has no expiry date. And sometimes, neither does curiosity.

She barely slept, her mind replaying fragments of old conversations and long-forgotten touches, snippets of college laughter, and the echo of her name in his voice.

Morning arrived, unkind and unforgiving. The pale morning light filtering through the curtains made everything look washed out, like the world itself was tired.

Tanvi woke up feeling like she hadn't slept at all. Her head throbbed, her eyes were puffy, and a dull ache settled in her lower back. The night had passed in a restless haze of scrolling, half-sleep, and intrusive memories.

Tarun was already up, making tea in the kitchen. The faint clink of cups and hiss of the gas stove reached her ears. She dragged herself out of bed, glancing at her phone – two unread messages from clients and a good morning text from Meghna. The baby shower. She sighed.

In the kitchen, Tarun noticed her sluggish steps and drawn face.

"You okay?" He asked, handing her a mug.

"Yeah... just didn't sleep well", she murmured, forcing a weak smile.

"Work stress?"

Tarun reached out, brushing a stray lock of hair behind her ear. "It'll settle."

If only he knew.

If only she understood it herself.

But some nights are like that – spent chasing ghosts through blue-lit screens and battling the echoes of what once was.

And Tanvi knew this was far from over.

"The ghosts you chase at night don't leave with the dawn."

Chapter – 7
The Echoes We Carry

The city was already awake by the time Tanvi and Tarun left home. A greyish morning sky hung low over Mumbai, and the streets were thick with early traffic. Tanvi sat in the passenger seat, a mug of half-finished coffee in hand, the bitter taste doing little to lift the fog in her head.

The Mumbai traffic was as usual chaotic – honking, hurried bikers weaving through the narrow gaps. Tanvi stared out of the window, her fingers absently picking at the hem of her *kurta*.

She felt exhausted. She hadn't slept. Not really.

The night had slipped through her fingers in a haze of scrolling, searching, stalking. It should have bored her. It didn't.

Why does she even care? Because he was the first person she loved. And someone who broke her.

But it was a lifetime ago.

Then why does it still ache?

"You okay?" Tarun asked, glancing sideways at her pale face.

"Yeah", she murmured, forcing a smile. "Just anxious."

He reached over, squeezed her hand, and for a moment, guilt gnawed at her. Tarun, steady and kind, was the one constant in her storm of scattered emotions. She didn't deserve this man. Not when a ghost from the past still had the power to unsettle her so completely.

The clinic was a bit colder than usual. The air was a mix of coffee aroma and cool air conditioning. They waited in the plush reception area, a TV playing muted music videos overhead. Tarun flipped through and old issue of National Geographic, pretending to read, while Tanvi kept glancing at the corridor leading to the embryology lab. Every time a figure in a lab coat passed by, her pulse spiked, her breath hitching for a second.

She hated herself for it.

You are here for your reports, for your future; not for a ghost from the past.

A nurse greeted them with a smile and handed over Tanvi's file. Dr Meera will call you in shortly. Tanvi flicked through the file, reading her reports and Tarun's. She could understand most of the reports by herself now - *Half a doctor, I am now*, that's how she jokes about it.

Amidst her thoughts, she heard a low laugh carried through from the corridor beyond the reception.

Deep. Warm. Familiar.

Her body went rigid.

That laugh.

She craned her neck toward the frosted glass doors, but the figure was obscured – a silhouette moving past, tall and broad-shouldered, the gait eerily familiar. Her pulse quickened, heart hammering against her ribs.

It's him.

Or maybe it's not.

Stop it, Tanvi.

The silhouette vanished around a corner, leaving her breathless.

"Tanvi?" Tarun's voice cut through her daze. "You okay?"

She swallowed hard. "Yeah. Just... I thought I saw someone I knew."

Before he could ask further, Dr Meera appeared. “Come in, both of you.” Tanvi gripped her file and followed Dr Meera to her room.

The consultation was a blur. It was the usual - follicle counts, hormone levels, AMH values.

“So, your hormone levels are stable, Tanvi”, Dr Meera began. “Tarun, your parameters are fine too. Overall a good baseline to move forward. We will start your ovarian stimulation from next week.” Her reassuring words about protocols and timelines were barely registered by Tanvi. Her mind refused to stay tethered to the present.

The meeting lasted another ten minutes – protocol plans, tentative retrieval dates, medication instructions. Through it all, Tanvi could barely focus. Her mind was fixated on the slight murmur of voices outside the frosted glass partition.

A male voice. Familiar. Low, measured, with a lilt she remembered from another life.

“Tanvi?” Tarun nudged her.

“Tanvi, any questions?” Dr Meera asked kindly.

She blinked. “Uh... no, I’m good.”

They left the room, and as they stepped into the corridor, Tanvi’s gaze involuntarily swept the lab’s glass door. A shadow moved behind it – tall, broad-shouldered, in scrubs.

She couldn't see his face.

Tarun was already halfway down the corridor, chatting with the receptionist about billing.

Tanvi lingered for a second longer. The figure inside turned away, his reflection merging with another technician's as they adjusted a microscope. She felt foolish, like a teenager spying on a long-lost crush.

Get a grip, she told herself.

She followed Tarun out.

Tarun gave her a puzzled glance as they stepped out. "You've been distracted all morning. Are you sure you're okay?"

"Yeah, just the nerves about the cycle", she replied.

He squeezed her shoulder. "We'll be fine. Let's go grab a bite."

She shook her head. "I'll head to the boutique. I have clients waiting. You go ahead."

They both left the clinic.

The boutique was quieter than usual that afternoon. Anisha was steaming a pastel saree at the back.

"Rough day?" Anisha asked, reading the exhaustion on her face.

"Long one", Tanvi replied, dropping her bag onto the counter.

Anisha grinned. "You know, sometimes the past finds funny ways of popping back into our lives. I ran into this guy from school the other day – total jerk back then, now all successful and charming. Life's weird, huh?"

Tanvi forced a laugh, though the words hit her harder than they should.

Yes, life was weird like that.

The day passed by with regular clients and endless discussions with masterji.

Evening bled into night, and Tanvi found herself back in her bedroom, phone in hand. She debated logging into Instagram again, checking if there were new stories or posts.

What are you hoping to find?

A notification pinged.

'Dr. Raghav Chaddha posted a new photo.'

She hesitated, her finger hovering over the screen.

Her heart drummed in her ears.

But this time...

She didn't open it.

She locked the phone, turned away, and forced herself to sleep.

Though the shadows of her past still clung to the edges of her mind.

Chapter – 8
A Belly Full of Wishes

Tanvi stood by the window of their bedroom, staring at the city skyline smeared in dusky oranges and deepening purples. She clutched the invitation card in her hand – 'Meghna's Baby Shower, This Sunday, 4 PM.' A cheerful pastel stork illustration grinned up at her, carrying a bundled baby in its beak. It was already five past five.

Tarun walked in, "Why aren't you ready?" he asked, eyeing the untouched *saree* she'd laid out on the bed.

"I don't feel like going", Tanvi murmured, not meeting his gaze.

"You should", he coaxed. "Meghna's your oldest friend. She called so many times. It might be a good change."

She wanted to argue, to curl up in bed and let the evening pass without her. But the thought of another lecture on 'staying positive' made her swallow the protest. She forced a smile instead. "Okay."

She dressed slowly. She wore a sea green *Paithani saree* she'd pulled from her boutique last evening, and paired it with delicate gold jewellery.

"You look beautiful", Tarun said as Tanvi stepped out of the bedroom, "just like a new bride". Tanvi offered a brief smile and stepped out of the house.

She booked an Ola to Meghna's house.

By the time, she reached the party was in full swing. A typical Maharashtrian *god bharai.*

Marigold garlands framed the doorway, their bright orange and yellow strands swaying gently in the breeze. Strings of mango leaves hung in perfect symmetry, and a rangoli bloomed in hues of pink, turquoise, and saffron at the entrance. Inside, the air smelled of jasmine and *ghee.* Women in vibrant *sarees* bustled about, their green glass bangles clinking softly as they arranged trays of sweets, *haldi-kumkum* platters, and coconut-filled *kalashas.*

Meghna sat on a low wooden platform, dressed in a rich purple *saree*, bangles stacked up to her elbows, a tiny *nath* adorning her nose, and a string of *mogras* in her hair, and her cheeks flushed with joy. The slight swell of her belly, accentuated by the drape of the *saree.*

"You look beautiful, Megs", Tanvi managed, leaning in for a careful hug.

"I'm so happy you came, Tanu. I was worried you'd be stuck with clients or something."

"Wouldn't miss it", Tanvi lied smoothly.

She handed Meghna a silk-wrapped gift – an indigo hand-embroidered maternity *kurta* from her boutique. Meghna's eyes glistened.

"This is beautiful, Tanu."

"You're going to be a beautiful mother, Megs", Tanvi whispered, hugging her tightly.

And for the first time that day, she let herself feel both things at once – the ache of her own emptiness and the fierce, loyal love she had for her oldest friend.

She and Meghna had spent countless summer afternoons during school days, gulping down cold *aam panna* and complaining about their teachers, dreams of travel and love spinning around them like silk threads.

"You know what I want, Tanu?" Meghna had asked one monsoon evening, the scent of wet earth hanging heavy in the air. "A fat wedding, a cute husband and a baby boy with your curls and my dimples."

They had giggled for hours, making imaginary lists of baby names and arguing over the best *modak* recipe.

Now, watching Meghna radiant on her *Dohale Jevan*, Tanvi realized – Meghna had gotten it all. The loving husband, the big wedding, the baby on the way.

And she...

She was still waiting.

Still carrying hopes, she was terrified to speak aloud.

The ache swelled in her chest like an old wound reopened. But she let the memory settle gently inside her.

The *Dohale Jevan* rituals began. An elderly aunt sang a folk song as another woman applied turmeric to Meghna's cheeks. The sound of conch shells and women's ululating cheers filled the room as a silver plate of fruits and sweets was presented.

Someone handed Tanvi a plate of *modaks* and *puran polis*, but she couldn't bring herself to eat.

She smiled, she laughed where expected, exchanged pleasantries, and passed compliments to the other women for their *sarees*.

But her heart wasn't there.

Everywhere she looked, there were rounded bellies and hopeful whispers of baby names, of nursery colours, of future birthdays. The air was thick with stories she no longer felt part of.

At one point, a little girl tugged at her hand, offering her a jasmine *gajra*. *"Aapke baalon mein laga do na, aunty."*

Tanvi forced a smile, taking the *gajra* and tucking it into her hair. "Thank you, sweetheart."

Across the room, Meghna giggled as her mother fed her sweetened milk. The women around clapped and teased about how the baby would look, whose eyes it would have, whether it would be a boy or a girl.

A part of Tanvi wanted to be happy – genuinely, selflessly happy. Meghna deserved this joy. But another part of her, the part that carried years of unspoken grief, ached bitterly.

Her phone buzzed in her clutch.

A message from Tarun:

"Hope it's going okay. Call me when you're done. Miss you."

She typed back a simple – *"Will do. Miss you too."*

Another round of ritual songs began. Tanvi slipped her phone away, composed herself, and stepped back into the circle of women.

An elderly neighbour approached, her voice syrupy sweet and sharp as glass.

"Beta, kab khushkhabri doge? Ab toh tumhari bhi baari hai."

The words landed like tiny darts, their sting familiar but still sharp.

Tanvi's throat tightened. She gave a polite nod and looked away, pretending to adjust her *saree*'s pleats. She excused herself from the group, and slipped into the guest bathroom.

The grief has come over again. She looked at herself in the mirror. The woman in the mirror looked pale, her kohl smudged slightly at the corners, hair dishevelled from the evening's chaos. A stranger.

Her phone again buzzed on the counter. She almost ignored it but habit made her glance down. A notification from the IVF clinic's app – a gentle reminder about tomorrow's scan and injection schedule.

The ache in her chest deepened. She gripped the sink. The city lights beyond the small window flickered like restless fireflies. Somewhere far away, a train whistle echoed.

Tanvi composed herself yet again, dabbed at her eyes, reapplied her lipstick, pasted a brave practiced smile and walked out of the washroom.

The rest of the evening rolled on in a blur of cheerful toasts, awkward games, and photo sessions. Tanvi drifted from group to group, sipping a watered-down orange juice she had no taste for, dodging conversations.

As the *Dohale Jevan* wound down, the women dispersed with their *haldi*-smeared cheeks and sweets packed dabbas. Meghna was now opening her presents. Soft toys, rattles, baby blankets, a tiny silver anklet set.

Tanvi gave a tight hug to Meghna before leaving. "You will be an incredible mother", she whispered and stepped out into the soft orange glow of dusk.

The air outside smelled of roasted peanuts. Mumbai's evening traffic had begun its restless dance. Honking autos, office-goers hurrying past, and endless lanes of cars.

She took an auto back home and let the city blur past.

Before she entered the house, she took a long breath and promised herself – **Tomorrow, I will let this go.**

Chapter – 9
Familiar Strangers

The pale blue walls of the IVF clinic had begun to feel eerily familiar. The same aroma, the quiet murmurs of nurses, the steady shuffle of patients waiting for their names to be called. The clinic felt colder than usual that morning. Or maybe it was just Tanvi's nerves, tightening with every step she took towards the reception.

"Good morning, ma'am", the receptionist greeted, recognizing Tanvi from her previous visits. "Please have a seat. Nurse Leena will assist you with your injections and scans."

Tanvi sat in the waiting area, a file clutched in her lap, watching the second hand of the wall clock move with agonizing slowness.

It will all begin again – the injections, the hormone rush, the routine of early morning scans. She'd imagined the physical pain would be the worst part, but it wasn't. It was the anticipation. The constant coil of hope and dread wound so tightly inside her chest that she could barely breathe.

Tarun wasn't with her today. A work meeting, he couldn't miss. He'd asked her twice if she'd be okay going alone, and she'd smiled, lied, and sent him off. He'd promised to join for the weekend scan.

Her phone buzzed – *'Ping me once you're done. Love you.'*

Tanvi typed a quick *'Will do'* and tucked the phone away.

"Tanvi Mehra", the nurse called.

She stood, smoothing down the creases of her *kurta* and followed her into the scan room.

She was familiar with the routine – transvaginal scans, the dreaded shots and occasional blood draws. The physical discomfort had dulled into a background ache; it wasn't the needles that hurt anymore. It was everything else.

The scan room was cool and dimly lit. Dr Meera greeted her with a practiced warmth.

"Good Morning dear, let's take a look at the ovaries before we begin."

Tanvi nodded, lying back on the examination table. The cold gel on the transvaginal probe made her flinch.

Dr Meera gently moved the probe and examined the ovaries one by one - first right and the left. "Looks good", she remarked. "Let's begin".

She jotted something on the yellow follicular monitoring sheet and instructed the sister - "Start with 300 U daily, next scan after five days."

Nurse Leena gave a silent nod.

Dr Meera turned to Tanvi, "Good luck Tanvi, I really hope PGT works for you guys. Let's think good and stay positive." Her words encouraging.

"Yes doctor, really hoping so." Tanvi replied softly.

As she lay on the examination table, the door opened — and in the soft shuffle of footsteps and murmur of papers being exchanged, she heard it. A voice.

A deep, steady voice, giving instructions to someone.

She couldn't see his face, but she knew. Every cell in her body knew.

Her pulse quickened, a cold sweat forming at the base of her neck. She tried to look, but the angle and the drawn curtain blocked her view.

"Okay, Tanvi. You're done", the nurse smiled. "Please wait outside for your instructions."

Tanvi dressed in silence, swallowing down the tight knot in her throat. Outside the scan room, she waited to collect her updated prescription.

That's when she saw him.

Across the hallway, near the embryology lab's glass-panelled door – Raghav.

It was unmistakable this time. No fleeting glimpse, no imagined voice. It was him, standing beside a nurse, a file in his hand, discussing something with another embryologist.

His face was sharper now, a little older, the faintest touch of grey at his temples. But the eyes – intense, dark eyes – hadn't changed. Neither had the way his jaw clenched when he was focused.

For a moment, Tanvi couldn't move. Her body went cold, a surreal numbness spreading through her limbs. She half-hoped that he wouldn't look up. And half-prayed that he would.

And then he did.

Their eyes met across the hallway.

Shock. Recognition. A jolt of something neither of them had words for.

Raghav's expression shifted in a fraction of a second – confusion giving way to disbelief, then something else. A memory resurrected too abruptly.

His mind reeled back. College. That monsoon-soaked July evening. The fight outside the old cafe. The sharp, irreversible rupture. The last message he'd sent before disappearing from her life.

He'd seen the name Tanvi on the patient list a week ago. But it hadn't clicked. The list read Tanvi Mehra. Back then – she was Tanvi Arora.

He looked down at the patient file now in his hand, and something shifted in his face. The name on the file said 'Tanvi Arora Mehra'. He hadn't connected the dots. But now, seeing her, reading her name, it was undeniable.

Fifteen years collapsed into that single, piercing moment.

Tanvi quickly turned her gaze away, pretending to look at the prescription papers, her heart pounding so violently she was sure it would burst.

Nurse Leena appeared beside Tanvi with a file. "Please collect your file from the reception, ma'am."

Tanvi turned away first. As she walked towards the reception, her hands shook. She didn't look back.

Raghav was still standing there, looking as if the ground had tilted under him.

The nurse called him for another case. He forced himself to move, to keep his expression neutral. But his pulse raced.

Tanvi left the clinic quickly. She needed to get out before her legs gave way.

In the car, she gripped the steering wheel tight, her knuckles white.

It wasn't over.

Fifteen years had not been enough.

Not even close.

The storm inside her was relentless. **The past wasn't done with her yet.**

And neither, it seemed, was Raghav.

Chapter – 10
Chaos and Clutter

The morning sunlight streamed through Tanvi's boutique, catching on sequins and silk, turning the small space into a kaleidoscope of colour. But to her, everything felt muted, hazy, like she was moving through fog.

The image of Raghav's face at the clinic clung to her thoughts, intrusive and insistent. A face both too familiar and too foreign now, edged with old memories and unresolved ache.

She barely registered her staff's greetings. She went straight to her desk, a steaming cup of chai left untouched by the side.

Orders needed finalizing. Fittings were scheduled. A bride's *lehenga* delivery was due by evening. But Tanvi's mind wouldn't settle. The swatches of fabric blurred, client names slipped from her memory, and her usually precise handwriting on the order forms looked hurried, uneven.

She snapped at Anisha over an appointment timing, only to realize she was the one who'd written it down wrong the day before.

By noon, the boutique's rhythm – usually a familiar, soothing chaos – had turned unbearable.

The phone rang – a client following up on her *sangeet* outfit. Tanvi answered, offering mechanical reassurances, only to realize halfway through the call that she was talking to the wrong person about the wrong order. Embarrassed, she fumbled an apology, promised to call back, and hung up with trembling fingers.

She turned to the tailor station where a pale pink *anarkali* meant for a baby shower was being packed in a blue box, meant for a different client.

"Are you people blind? That's not hers!" She burst out, startling everyone.

The room went silent. The hum of the sewing machines, the rustle of silk – everything paused.

"Sorry, ma'am", a junior staffer mumbled, hastily correcting it.

Anisha exchanged glances with the other girls. Tanvi was always particular, organized, and patient. Today, she was sharp-edged, brittle.

Tanvi closed her eyes, mortified at her own outburst. This wasn't her. She wasn't this woman snapping at people over a misplaced box. She retreated to her small office at the back, the scent of fabric glue and freshly steamed clothes chasing her. Shutting the door behind her, she leaned against it, taking a shaky breath.

She opened her phone out of habit. No new messages from Tarun. A notification from the IVF clinic about medication reminders.

She swiped it away quickly, but the damage was done. The memory of his face, the rush of old emotions, the messy tangle of grief and anger and unfinished conversations surged forward.

What was she supposed to do now? Her mind spun in confusion. Should she stop the treatment at this clinic altogether? How will she explain that to Tarun? And if she stayed, how would she face Raghav? A thousand questions crashed through her thoughts, each one heavier than the last, leaving her overwhelmed and restless.?

A knock at the door.

"Ma'am? The bride's here for her trial."

Tanvi smoothed her hair and dabbed a tissue at the corner of her eyes.

"Coming," she called out, forcing her voice steady.

She glanced at her reflection in the glass cabinet – tired, frayed, but still standing.

Chaos and clutter. That's what her boutique looked like today. That's what her heart felt like.

She stepped out of the office, pasted on a professional smile, and dove back into the day's demands.

Across the city, in a glass-walled embryology lab, Raghav felt lost too. He sat at his desk, the glow of his monitor reflecting off his glasses. Embryology records lined up in neat rows, yet everything swam before his eyes – day3/day5 embryos, grades – a language he spoke fluently, but today it all blurred.

He mechanically scrolled through the patients list for next day's scan, half-dreading, half-anticipating another glimpse of her name. When it didn't appear, a strange mixture of relief and disappointment tightened his chest.

Ira, his junior embryologist, entered with embryo culture details.

"Leave it. I'll review it later", Raghav muttered.

He never left things for later. But today, it was all different.

The lab manager approached Raghav.

"Sir, Mrs. Malik's blastocyst grading has discrepancies between your sheet and Ira's."

A careless oversight. One he'd have caught instantly any other day.

"Correct it", Raghav muttered, rubbing his temples.

His notes were smudged, numbers off. His famously meticulous handwriting looked hurried, uneven.

His hands were unsteady as he signed off reports. He looked confused, not his usual self. The usual calm on his face was a chaos today.

His junior staff exchanged cautious glances, wondering what was wrong.

He stepped out of the lab into the clinic's corridor, eyes closed against the relentless ache in his head. It wasn't the fatigue of a long day or the steady hum of the clinic chaos – it was something much deeper, older. A wound he thought time had sealed, now cracked open in an instant.

He hated how easily his mind betrayed him, dragging him back to those days. College. Reckless, defiant, and desperately in love. He could still picture her – Tanvi – all fire and softness, with a smile that disarmed him and a stubborn streak that matched his own. They had been inseparable, clinging to each other like lifelines in a world that felt too wide, too uncertain.

And then it broke. Not with a fight, not with words, but with a single mistake, a truth they were both too young and too scared to face. He remembered the arguments, the silences.

And now, here she was. In his clinic, in his world again. He clenched his jaw, willing his heart to behave, trying to silence the voice inside that whispered of what they'd lost. This wasn't the time for sentiment. He was the embryologist, she was a patient, that's it. That was the boundary, the rule. Yet the ache in his chest told him that the past didn't care for rules.

He opened his eyes slowly, exhaling a sharp, bitter breath. Damn it. The past was supposed to stay buried. And yet here it was – raw, alive, and staring him right in the face.

From somewhere nearby, a lullaby played on a phone – a pregnant woman waiting for her scan.

He leaned against the cold wall. His hands trembled against the cool plaster, and for a moment, he hated how weak he felt. He needed to pull himself together before anyone could see him like this.

He left early, for the first time in years.

He stepped into the gathering dusk, lit a cigarette – a habit he'd abandoned long ago, but today he needed one – he let the smoke curl into the humid air.

In different corners of the restless city:

Both Tanvi and Raghav promised themselves the same thing,

Tomorrow, I'll let this go.

Or at least try.

Some days unravel without warning. Threads you thought were tight, slipping loose, tangling into knots you can't unknot.

Chapter – 11
Frayed Edges

The days blurred into each other – a dizzying routine of early morning injections, follicular scans, and bruised skin. The clinic's sterile white corridors had become too familiar, the antiseptic chill lingering in the bones. The soft murmur of nurses discussing estradiol levels and follicle sizes looped endlessly in the background, a language Tanvi now understood well.

Physically, it wasn't unbearable. A dull ache in her lower abdomen, a prick here and there, the discomfort of bloating from hormones. But emotionally, it was a relentless storm. Every visit to the clinic was a reminder of how fragile hope could be, how each number on the scan or blood report carried the power to either lift her up or shatter her.

The nights were the hardest. The mind, even exhausted, refused to rest. Sleep arrived in stolen fragments, only to be chased away by a rogue memory that clawed its way to the surface.

Back at the boutique, things weren't any better. The bridal season rush was relentless, and the usually steady rhythm of fittings and deliveries began to fray. Designs that once brought her joy now felt like tasks to tick-off on a never-ending list.

Anisha, her reliable assistant, approached Tanvi one afternoon, her face pale and drawn, eyes rimmed red.

"Ma'am... I need to talk."

Tanvi looked up from a stack of fabric swatches, sensing the heaviness in the girl's voice.

"My mom's not well. She's been admitted again... I'll need to go home for a while. Maybe a week... maybe more."

Tanvi's stomach twisted. Of course, she couldn't say no – Anisha had been nothing but her anchor through many stormy seasons. But the timing couldn't have been worse.

"I'm so sorry, Ani. Go, be with her. Don't worry about here... we'll manage somehow", Tanvi said, forcing a reassuring smile, while something inside her cracked a little more.

Anisha's eyes glistened. "Thank you, ma'am."

And just like that, one more thread in Tanvi's fragile safety net gave way.

No sooner had Anisha left than another storm rolled in. A difficult client, a wealthy bride's mother, stormed into the boutique, her voice sharp and shrill.

"This is not the shade of gold we approved! I won't pay for this nonsense!"

Tanvi's temples throbbed. The fabric was the exact shade. She knew it. But there was no point arguing. Apologies were made, and alterations were promised. The woman left in a huff, and the boutique air felt heavier, thickened with tension and frayed tempers.

That evening, Tarun noticed it. The tight lines on Tanvi's face, the weary slump of her shoulders as she stepped into the apartment.

"Come here", he said softly from the couch, his arms opening for her like a refuge.

She sank beside him on the couch, her head resting on his shoulder.

"You can't keep going like this, Tan. You're running on empty."

"I'm fine", she lied.

"No, you're not. Between the treatments, the boutique, everything... you need a break."

If only he knew about the ghost too. The name she hadn't uttered, but that haunted the peripheries of every quiet moment.

She closed her eyes. "I can't, Tarun. The IVF cycle is moving fast, the eggs would be retrieved in less than a week, Then the PGT reports will take another ten to twelve days. Then decisions. It's not the time."

Life had never felt so fragile.

"Exactly", he said. "So once the retrieval's done and we're just waiting, let's get out of here. Just for a couple of days. Lonavala, Alibaug, anywhere. Somewhere without needles, Wi-Fi, or fabric swatches."

She smiled faintly, the idea both tempting and terrifying. She hadn't left the city in months.

"I'll think about it."

"Promise me."

"I promise."

The promise was hollow, but it was something.

Later that night, after Tarun had drifted into a gentle snore beside her, Tanvi lay awake. The ceiling fan hummed a lullaby, but sleep remained a stranger.

Her phone screen glowed in the dim light as she absentmindedly scrolled through old pictures – birthdays, boutique launches, their wedding in Udaipur, and then, a folder titled "Getaways".

A photo caught her eye.

A misty morning in Lonavala, her hair wet with drizzle, Tarun grinning in the background, holding two cups of steaming cutting chai.

She let out a breath she hadn't realised she was holding. Maybe a break wouldn't be so bad.

For a few moments, the weight in her chest loosened. She imagined the scent of rain-soaked earth, the cool wind on her face, the quiet away from clinics and clients and ghosts of the past.

Her eyes fluttered shut, phone still in hand.

The ache didn't disappear. But it dulled.

Just enough to let sleep find her.

Some wounds heal, some stay raw beneath the skin, and some you learn to stitch up each morning before the world sees them.

Chapter – 12
The Unspoken Encounter

The procedure was done.

Tanvi drifted back to consciousness in the recovery room, the faint antiseptic scent mingling with the distant hum of machines. The pale blue curtains around her bed swayed gently as a nurse adjusted the IV. Her lower abdomen ached with a dull, persistent heaviness, but the worst part wasn't the physical pain – it was still the storm whirling in her chest.

Tarun was by her side, his face drawn but relieved. He reached out, touching her head gently.

"It's done, are you okay?"

Tanvi gave him a faint, tired smile.

"How many?" She whispered, her throat dry.

Before Tarun could answer, a figure appeared at the foot of her bed. A man in a white coat, a tablet in hand, his face partly obscured by a surgical mask.

It was him.

Even through the mask, even beneath the cap, she recognized those eyes – the sharp, warm brown of a memory she'd tried to bury. A memory of a monsoon evening, rain tracing lazy patterns on foggy glass, his voice low and urgent as he'd whispered her name.

The years between them seemed to collapse in that instant, an unsaid current passing through the room.

Raghav's face, composed and professional, flickered with recognition. A moment of something raw, something neither of them could name.

He cleared his throat and then glanced briefly at the tablet, then at her, his voice clipped, professional.

"Mrs. Tanvi Mehra", he began, voice even, detached. "The egg retrieval went smoothly. We retrieved eleven oocytes. The quality appears good on initial assessment."

Tanvi felt her throat go dry. She managed a stiff nod. "Okay."

"Your husband's sample has been processed as well. Fertilization will be attempted today, and we'll monitor for embryo formation over the next 3–5 days."

Another pause. The air felt dense with everything they weren't saying.

He glanced down at his tablet again, and for a second, his fingers lingered against the edge of the screen. "The lab will keep you updated", he added.

"Thank you", Tanvi said softly.

Their eyes met, and in that gaze – there was everything. The unfinished stories, the buried questions, the lives lived apart, and now this inexplicable crossing of paths.

Neither acknowledged the past. Neither let the tremor in their voices linger. It was an interaction two strangers could have had – but they both knew better.

Tarun thanked him with a polite smile, oblivious to the history thick in the room's sterile air.

Raghav gave a quick nod and walked away. His shoulders stiff, his steps measured.

And just before he stepped out, Tanvi saw it – a slight falter in his stride. A moment of hesitation. But he kept walking, the door clicking softly shut behind him.

And just like that, he was gone.

Tanvi exhaled, only realizing then how tightly she'd been clutching the bedsheet.

Tarun looked at Tanvi, smiled, and slipped his hand into hers. "Told you, you're stronger than you think."

But inside her, Tanvi knew strength wasn't the problem. It was the ghosts you carried while pretending to be strong.

And today, one of them had a name. A face. And had spoken to her.

Later that evening

Back home, the apartment felt unusually quiet. The dim light from the living room lamp cast soft shadows on the walls. Tanvi lay curled up on the sofa, a hot water bag pressed to her abdomen. Tarun had ordered her favourite soup – tomato and basil – but it sat untouched on the table.

The physical ache was manageable. The real pain was somewhere deeper, gnawing, refusing to settle.

Tarun sat beside her, scrolling through his phone absentmindedly.

"We'll get the fertilization report tomorrow", he said, trying to sound upbeat. Once the embryos are ready and PGT is scheduled – we'll have a few days before transfer, right?"

Tanvi nodded, eyes fixed on the ceiling.

"Let's get away for the weekend, away from this chaos."

Tanvi blinked, turning toward him.

"Where would we go?"

"Lonavala? It's close. Quick drive. Fresh air. Just... us."

A fragile smile touched her lips. The thought of winding roads, mist-laced hills, and the faint smell of wet earth made her chest ache in a different way.

"Yeah. It'll be good for us. Clear our heads before... everything else." Tarun added.

Tanvi closed her eyes for a moment, picturing it. The quiet. The escape. The illusion of normalcy.

"I'd like that", she murmured.

Tarun leaned in, brushing his lips against her temple. "We'll book something. Maybe that old resort we stayed at two years ago? With the lake view?"

She nodded, her throat tight.

Neither of them said it out loud, but both were nervous. The PGT results would decide everything – which embryos would survive, which ones would be normal, which would have a chance. Hope was a dangerous thing. Yet, here they were, clinging to it.

Tarun scrolled through his phone and held it out. "This one okay?" He asked, showing her a picture of the cottage overlooking the misty hills.

Tanvi's lips curved faintly.

"Perfect."

She felt the warmth of his hand in hers and realized how much she needed this. Not just the getaway. But the permission to pause. To breathe.

And for the first time in days, she allowed herself to hope that maybe – just maybe – she could carry both.

The pain.

And the hope.

As Tarun switched off the lights and slid beside her, Tanvi rested her head on his shoulder. The city hummed quietly outside their window. And as sleep pulled at the edges of her exhaustion, she clung to one fragile thought.

Tomorrow would come. And with it, another chance to hold on.

Chapter – 13
The Pause Between Storms

The hills of Lonavala were veiled in a soft, persistent mist as the car climbed the winding roads. The air smelt of wet earth and pine needles, that oddly nostalgic scent of monsoon-soaked soil that always reminded Tanvi of childhood summers and simpler, lighter days.

Tarun drove in silence, one hand on the wheel, the other fiddling with the radio dial until an old Kishore Kumar classic played low in the background. Neither of them spoke much. And yet, the quiet didn't feel oppressive – it felt necessary, like the space between breaths.

Tanvi leaned her forehead against the cool windowpane, watching droplets race down the glass. The ache in her lower abdomen had dulled to a manageable throb, but the ache in her chest was harder to ignore.

"Okay?" Tarun asked softly, glancing sideways.

She nodded. "Better."

It wasn't a lie. It wasn't the truth either. It was somewhere in between – like most things in her life lately.

The Resort

They checked into a small, weathered cottage-style room overlooking the lake. The air smelled of rain-drenched wood and distant bonfire smoke. Tanvi dropped her bag near the door and stepped out onto the balcony. The view made her throat tighten – the mist rising off the water, the faint outline of trees blurred by fog.

"This is lovely", Tarun said, joining her. His hand brushed against hers. She didn't pull away.

For a brief moment, she let herself believe it could be just another getaway, like it used to be. Before hospital corridors and injections and reports with strange acronyms like AMH and PGT-A had hijacked their world.

The next morning, the rain had eased to a faint drizzle. They found a small, local cafe that served steaming plates of *poha* and cutting *chai* in chipped glass tumblers. Tanvi sipped the hot, oversweet tea and allowed herself to smile at Tarun's terrible joke about the world's soggiest *vada*.

After breakfast, they wandered aimlessly along a wooded trail behind the resort. The ground was soft, blanketed in wet leaves. Tarun picked up a stick and pretended it was a sword, challenging an invisible opponent.

"You're such a child", she laughed, a sound she hadn't heard from herself in weeks.

"Still got you to laugh though."

He snapped a selfie of them, rain-speckled, grinning. For a heartbeat, it felt easy. They spent hours walking and exploring the resort. Tarun continued cracking the lame jokes and Tanvi continued teasing him for being such a child.

In the late afternoon, while Tarun took a work call, Tanvi made her way to the lakeside alone. The water was dark, reflecting the restless sky. A pair of ducks cut ripples across the surface.

She sat on an old bench, the wood damp beneath her, and took out the leather-bound diary she'd impulsively thrown into her bag. The pages smelled faintly of old paper. She stared at the blank page for a long time before the words came:

"I don't know if I'll be a mother.

But I know I am surviving.

I am carrying the weight of hope and grief like twin stones in my chest."

A raindrop splashed onto the page, smudging the ink. She didn't bother wiping it away. She just closed it and placed it back in her tote as if trying to store the memory of the moment.

Across the shore, a young couple was taking pictures- different poses, all angles. It reminded Tanvi of how carefree and fun-loving she and Tarun were before all this began.

Evening Conversations

Back in the room, Tarun handed her a cup of hot chocolate, extra marshmallows floating lazily on top. They curled up under a shared blanket, the rain pattering softly against the glass.

"Remember when we made that list of baby names the year we got married?" Tarun asked suddenly, a wistful smile on his face.

Tanvi chuckled. "You wanted 'Kabir' if it was a boy. I wanted 'Anvi' for a girl."

"I still like Kabir."

"I still like Anvi."

They fell silent. The names hovered between them like ghosts of an alternate life.

"I don't know what the PGT report will say", Tarun murmured, his voice barely audible. "But whatever happens... I don't want us to forget how to be 'us'."

Tanvi rested her head on his shoulder. The warmth of his hand in hers felt like an anchor in a storm.

Later that night, long after Tarun had drifted into sleep, Tanvi lay awake, listening to the steady rhythm of rain on the cottage roof. The shadows on the ceiling shifted gently.

She felt the ache in her chest, the jagged pull of fear and hope. But for the first time in weeks, she let herself unclench – even if just a little.

Because in this quiet space between everything they'd lost and everything that might still be taken from them, she had found a kind of fragile peace.

And maybe – maybe that was enough for now.

The next morning, the hills were washed clean by the night's rain. A faint chill hung in the air as mist drifted over the lake. Tanvi packed her bag slowly, reluctant to leave the bubble of quiet they'd found in these two days.

As she zipped up her duffel, her phone buzzed on the nightstand. It was a message from Diksha – an old college friend, one of the few who knew about Tanvi's struggle with infertility. The words on the screen made her stomach drop.

"Lost the baby, Tanvi. Five months. Don't know how to breathe."

Tanvi sat down heavily on the edge of the bed. Her throat tightened, grief and anger and helplessness spiralling inside her. She knew those words. Knew that kind of hollow ache.

"What is it?" Tarun asked from the doorway, his brow furrowed.

"Diksha... she... she lost the baby."

Tarun's face softened. "I'm so sorry."

Tanvi inhaled shakily, then nodded. "I think I'll go meet her when we're back. She shouldn't be alone."

She didn't say it, but in that moment, she understood with aching clarity how pain recognized pain – how grief wasn't a contest, but a bond. And perhaps, in offering Diksha comfort, she might find a small, steadying thread to hold on to herself.

Tarun placed a hand on her shoulder. "Let's head back."

And as they drove down the winding hill road, Tanvi kept her phone in her lap, ready to text Diksha when she reached.

Ready, for once, to be the one offering warmth instead of seeking it.

Chapter – 14
The Shared Grief

The city felt heavier when they returned.

Mumbai's relentless hum – the traffic, the voices, the ceaseless rhythm of a place that didn't stop for anyone's sorrow – pressed in on Tanvi the moment they crossed the flyover. The memory of mist and lake water felt like something from another life.

She texted Diksha the moment she got home. "Can I come over?"

Diksha's reply was instant. "Please. I need you."

At Diksha's House

Diksha's apartment was dim, the curtains drawn against the harsh afternoon light. The air inside smelled faintly of lavender and something burnt in the kitchen.

Diksha sat curled on the couch, hair uncombed, her eyes puffy and raw.

The sight of her made Tanvi's heart twist. Not in pity – but in recognition.

"Hey", Tanvi whispered.

Diksha managed a broken smile. "I look like shit."

"You look like someone who's allowed to look like shit."

Diksha rested her head on Tanvi 's shoulder and for a long time, neither of them spoke. The silence was thick, but not uncomfortable. Tanvi let it settle, remembering how much she'd hated empty platitudes after her own failed cycles. Words rarely mattered. Presence did.

Finally, Diksha spoke. "I didn't even get to hold her. Five months, and they told me it was better this way... What does 'better' even mean, Tanvi?"

Tanvi's throat tightened. She reached for Diksha's hand. "I wish I could tell you. I've asked myself that a hundred times."

Diksha squeezed her fingers. "It doesn't go away, does it?"

"No", Tanvi admitted softly. "But you learn to breathe around it. Not through it – around it."

They sat like that, two women stitched together by invisible scars. Neither one offered easy answers, because neither believed in them anymore.

As dusk fell outside, Diksha fell asleep, her head on Tanvi's shoulder. Tanvi stayed there, watching the soft rise and fall of her friend's breath, realizing how grief didn't isolate people as much as it disguised itself in different forms – miscarriages, failed cycles, empty nurseries, aching silences.

And in that quiet living room, with the muted city beyond the window, Tanvi felt a strange, steadying calm. Not because things were better. But because, for once, she didn't feel alone in her unspoken ache.

The sky had already darkened by the time Tanvi left Diksha. The city outside was awash with the glitter of headlights and the soft haze of post-rain humidity clinging to the windows.

As she entered her apartment, she kicked off her shoes, dropped her bag by the door, and stood for a moment, letting the silence settle around her.

Tarun appeared from the kitchen, a cup of tea in hand. His face was a careful mixture of concern and caution – as if unsure how much space to offer her tonight.

"How was Diksha?" He asked gently.

Tanvi sighed, setting down her phone on the counter. "Broken. Angry. Half-alive."

Tarun nodded, his expression tightening. "I'm sorry."

"She fell asleep on my shoulder", Tanvi said, a small, sad smile flickering across her lips. "I didn't move. She just... needed someone there."

There was a pause, the kind that filled itself with all the words neither of them said aloud.

Then Tarun cleared his throat, running a hand through his hair. "The clinic called."

Tanvi's heart stuttered. The room seemed to narrow around her. "And?"

"They said fertilization went well. Seven embryos progressed to blastocysts and PGT was done. Results will take 10-12 days."

Seven. The number felt fragile and terrifyingly hopeful at once.

Tanvi swallowed hard. "Okay."

Tarun crossed the room and took her hand. "Whatever happens, we're still us."

And though she couldn't quite trust his voice, Tanvi nodded. She let her head rest briefly against his chest, feeling the steady thud of his heartbeat. It didn't erase the ache, or the ghosts, or the memories of hospital rooms and loss – hers, Diksha's, all the unnamed women she'd met in waiting rooms.

But for now, it was enough.

They spent the rest of the evening in quiet company, watching an old film neither of them paid attention to, Tarun occasionally reaching for her hand, Tanvi leaning against him. And sometime during the movie they both fell asleep.

Surprisingly, Tanvi slept peacefully that night.

And she realised, some nights weren't meant for fixing things. Some nights were only meant for surviving.

Chapter – 15
Pickle

The next day stretched endlessly.

Tanvi woke before dawn, the sky outside still a deep, bruised indigo. She lay in bed listening to the city gradually wake – the milkman's whistle, the clatter of newspaper deliveries, the faint hum of traffic returning to life.

The ache in her abdomen had faded, but a new heaviness sat in her chest. Today wasn't a regular day. Today marked the start of another long wait.

Tarun made her tea without asking, just the way she liked it – barely sweet, extra ginger. He placed the cup beside her and kissed the top of her head.

"Big day", he said quietly.

Tanvi gave him a wan smile. "Feels like waiting for exam results in school. Only... worse. And the results don't even come today."

The Waiting

Dr Meera had explained them the evening before. "The embryos are now frozen. PGT reports take around 10 to 12 days – we need to culture cells, analyse the DNA, confirm chromosomal status. Once we have the report, we'll call you."

It was the kind of wait Tanvi knew too well by now.

A stretch of days where time slowed, where every phone ring jolted her nerves, where hope and dread took turns gnawing at her insides.

Tarun went back to work, but made a point to check in every few hours. Tanvi tried keeping her boutique running, though she often found herself lost mid-conversation with a client, forgetting what fabric they'd asked for.

At night, she and Tarun curled up on the couch, watching mindless shows neither of them cared about. Neither spoke of numbers, embryos, or possibilities. It was a fragile, unspoken truce.

And just like that, somewhere in between waiting, hopes, and fears, the days passed by.

Ten days.

Then eleven.

Each one of the days dragging and rushing by in equal measure. And finally, on the twelfth day Tanvi received the much-awaited call.

Her phone buzzed in the afternoon while she was sitting in her boutique. She stared at the screen for a long moment – before swiping to answer.

"Hi Tanvi, we have your PGT report."

Her heart hammered.

"We tested seven embryos as we had told you", the doctor said, her tone professional but soft around the edges. "Six showed chromosomal abnormalities. Only one embryo came back euploid – genetically normal." Dr Meera added, "Please visit the clinic so that we can plan the transfer cycle."

Tanvi clutched the edge of the reception desk, the world blurring around her.

One.

Just one.

She ended the call and stood in the boutique, her pulse thudding in her ears. The dusky orange glow of the evening sun poured in through the glass door, catching motes of dust in its path.

Seven dreams had shrunk to one.

She walked outside, the evening breeze cooling her face. The city moved around her in its usual, indifferent way – car horns, street vendors calling out, a toddler wailing in the building next door. The world didn't pause for heartbreak. It never did.

Tanvi leaned against the railing of her boutique's entrance, staring at the streaked sky.

Is one enough?

She didn't know. She wasn't sure if anyone ever did.

But it was what they had.

After a long debate inside her head, she dialled Tarun's number. Tarun picked up on the first ring.

"Tanvi?"

"There's one," she said, barely able to get the words out. "Only one."

A beat of silence. Then his voice – steady, sure, almost a whisper. "One's enough."

Tears pricked her eyes before she could stop them.

"Yeah," she whispered. "One's enough."

That evening, by the time Tarun got home, the city had darkened into night, the distant hum of traffic a constant in the background. He stepped in, dropped his laptop bag by the door, and crossed the room in three quick strides.

Tanvi didn't speak – she just walked into his arms.

For a long time, they stood like that. No words, no brave smiles, no forced optimism. Just two people clinging to each other in a world that refused to promise them certainty.

After a while, Tarun spoke, his chin resting against her hair. "I know it's not what we hoped. But it's a chance."

Tanvi pulled back slightly, her fingers still twisted into the fabric of his shirt. "It scares me. Having only one. Like it has to carry everything now... all our hope. All our heartbreak. Everything."

He cupped her face in his hands, thumb brushing away a tear she hadn't noticed. "Then let's name it."

She blinked up at him.

"What?"

"Let's give this one a name", he said softly. "So, it's not just a number on a chart or a stat in a report. So, it's ours, whatever happens."

Tanvi let out a shaky breath, something between a sob and a laugh. "What would we call it?"

Tarun shrugged, a faint smile playing on his lips. "Hope? Magic? Something weird like Pickle, because it's tiny and we don't know if it'll stick."

Tanvi laughed through the ache in her chest. "Pickle?"

"Could be anything. As long as it's ours."

She leaned into him again, her voice muffled against his chest. "Okay. Pickle it is."

And in that small, ridiculous, fragile decision, the heaviness eased a little. Not gone, but softened.

They didn't know what the next cycle would bring. Or what the next phone call might say. But tonight, they had one embryo. And it had a name.

And sometimes, that was enough.

Later that night, they sat on the balcony with mugs of chamomile tea, the city stretched out beneath them in a patchwork of yellow lights and restless traffic. Neither spoke much. The kind of silence that isn't heavy – just shared.

Somewhere in the distance, a dog barked, a siren wailed, and the night rolled on as it always did.

Tanvi leaned her head on Tarun's shoulder. His arm tightened around her, and for the first time in what felt like months, she didn't feel entirely alone in the weight she carried.

"One's enough", he said again, almost to himself.

Tanvi didn't answer. She let her gaze drift to the sky, searching for a star that wasn't there, and thought about how even the smallest lights were still lights.

Pickle.

Their one chance.

And for tonight – with tired hearts and hopeful, breakable hands – it would have to be enough.

The night hummed on, indifferent and vast.

And somewhere in a lab, on a frozen straw, a tiny hope waited - PICKLE!

Chapter – 16
The Gravity of Glances

The clinic looked exactly as it always did – pale blue walls, faux plants near the entrance, the soft click of nurses' shoes echoing in the corridor. But something about walking in this time felt different. Heavier.

Tanvi tightened her grip around the brown file, her name scribbled in bold marker on its cover, as if ownership over her heartbreak had to be declared. She took her usual seat by the reception, facing the long corridor towards the doctor's room.

Across from her, a woman in her late thirties sat clutching a report envelope, her eyes rimmed with a kind of exhaustion Tanvi knew too well. A young couple whispered to each other in hushed, hopeful tones. The waiting room was filled with people teetering between hope and grief, trying to make peace with their odds.

The nurse finally called her name.

Inside, Dr Meera's face was the same practiced mix of professionalism and warmth. "Good Morning Tanvi, hope you had a good break." She spoke gently while she did her sonography.

"Your scan looks good. The lining is thin, as expected at baseline. We'll start you on estrogen from today. We'll review the endometrial thickness around day 10. If all goes well, we'll plan the embryo transfer by day 15."

Tanvi nodded, absorbing the words like a lecture she already knew by heart. The dates. The numbers. The markers to watch for.

"Any questions?"

"Only one", Tanvi managed, voice tighter than she intended. "Is one enough?"

The doctor's expression softened, a glimmer of empathy behind her lenses. "Sometimes one is all it takes."

Tanvi swallowed the lump rising in her throat. She offered a polite thank you and made her way out.

And as she turned the corner, moving toward the pharmacy counter, she saw him.

Raghav.

Clipboard in hand, walking alongside a junior embryologist, deep in discussion about a protocol. His voice, that familiar low timbre, sent a current of something sharp through her chest before she could even process his face.

And then he looked up.

For a moment, the world stilled. The air between them thickened, not with words, but with everything that had been left unsaid.

A flicker of recognition in his eyes. A faint, polite nod. "Hi."

Tanvi's throat constricted. It was ridiculous how that one word, so ordinary, could scrape old wounds open. She forced a stiff, tight-lipped "Hi" in return.

He kept walking. So did she.

But the knot in her chest didn't loosen. With the heavy heart and lingering thoughts, she drove to her boutique.

The boutique was unusually silent today, not many clients.

Tanvi was mindlessly scrolling through her Instagram when the WhatsApp notification popped up from an unknown number.

"Hey. I know this is unexpected. But I think we need to talk. Some unfinished conversations that I need to get out of my system. Would you... would you meet me? Just for a coffee. There's a Café Coffee Day across from the clinic. No pressure. I understand if you don't want to...but I really hope that we can meet..."

Raghav

Tanvi's stomach flipped.

She read the message once. Then twice. A surge of heat bloomed beneath her skin – anger, confusion, curiosity. She wanted to throw the phone aside, pretend it didn't matter.

But it did.

Because some people don't leave quietly.

Some ghosts sit in your chest, waiting for a crack in your resolve.

She typed, I don't think it's a good idea.

Deleted it.

Wrote, I don't want to open old wounds.

Deleted that too.

Her fingers hovered over the screen before she finally typed:

Okay. Maybe next time when I am coming for the scan.

And before she could second-guess herself, she hit send.

Raghav: *Thank you.*

The reply came within seconds.

Tanvi leaned her head at the table and closed her eyes.

What are you doing, Tanvi? Her mind questioned.

But some stories don't end just because you stop talking about them.

Some things have to be spoken aloud before they can be laid to rest.

And maybe this was that.

Maybe it was time to treat the wounds from the past.

That evening, by the time Tanvi got home, the house smelled of something warm and familiar – Tarun was in the kitchen, heating up dal and rice, a small attempt at normalcy in a life where very little felt normal anymore.

He looked up when she entered, a tired smile softening his face. "Hey! How did it go?"

Tanvi shrugged, setting her file on the dining table. "Baseline's fine. Estrogen starts today. Tentative plan for transfer in two weeks."

He crossed the room and pulled her into a hug, resting his chin on her head. "Good. That's good."

She held him, feeling the steady thud of his heartbeat beneath her ear. The comfort of it. The weight of it.

And the guilt.

Because she planned to be sitting across a table from a man she'd never expected to see again – a man whose name she hadn't spoken in years. A man who still held the shape of her past.

And Tarun had no idea.

She could've told him. Maybe should've. But how do you explain a storm you don't fully understand yourself?

So, she stayed quiet.

Later, as they ate dinner in front of the TV, both pretending to watch a show neither was following, Tanvi's phone buzzed again. A reminder notification, Raghav: "Can't wait to see you".

She quickly swiped it away before Tarun could see.

And when he reached out to tuck a strand of hair behind her ear, smiling in that weary, hopeful way of his, she forced herself to smile back.

Some truths could wait a few more days.

Chapter – 17
Between Past and Present

Tanvi's follow-up scan was due today. But it wasn't the scan that made her palms clammy or her pulse race. She stood in front of the mirror, clothes strewn across the bed like silent witnesses to her turmoil, unable to decide what to wear.

What to wear? She asked herself for the fifth time.

I'm going to the clinic for a follow-up, not on some date, her mind argued.

But her heart – foolish and stubborn wouldn't stop pounding. She wanted to look her best. Cover the fine lines, the soft weight gathered over fifteen years, the traces of lost time. She felt like a college girl dressing up to meet her secret crush.

Finally, she reached for a long, flowy white dress with delicate floral embroidery along the hem. A dress is easier for the scan, she told herself. Though she knew there were other reasons too, ones she wasn't quite ready to admit.

"Wow... you look fresh and lovely", Tarun said as he stepped out of the washroom, towel around his neck. "Haven't seen you wear white in years."

"Should I drop you to the clinic on my way?"

"Thanks, but I'll drive myself. Need to run a few errands before the appointment", Tanvi replied, avoiding his gaze, fussing with her bag's strap.

The clinic was its usual self – a cocktail of hope and fear hanging in the air. But today, those emotions clung to her skin differently.

She saw Raghav the moment she stepped in, as though he'd been waiting for her in that corridor.

A second later, her phone buzzed.

"Will wait at the café. See you once you're done."

Tanvi stared at the message, then glanced at Raghav – confused, unsure if she should go.

The scan went smoothly. Her endometrial lining was perfect. Dr Meera advised a few hormonal tests before scheduling the transfer.

As her blood was being drawn in the phlebotomy room, a battle raged inside her – between mind and heart, between reason and longing.

And, as it always did, her heart won.

I'll be quick, she told herself, grabbed her bag, and left the clinic.

The Café

The soft jingle of the café bell felt impossibly loud as Tanvi stepped inside, her heart pounding a nervous, unsteady rhythm against her ribs. The air was warm, thick with the scent of freshly ground coffee and sugar, but inside her, a cold ache had settled.

She saw him almost immediately.

Raghav sat by the window, the fading daylight throwing soft, broken shadows across his face. His eyes met hers – steady, unreadable – as if trying to measure how much time had passed, how much they had changed.

She managed a brief, measured, "Hey", and slid into the chair opposite him.

"Thank you for coming", Raghav said softly, his voice pitched low enough for only her to hear. His gaze lingered, a trace of something old and familiar surfacing. "You look... lovely."

Tanvi gave a small nod. "I wasn't sure I would... but here I am."

He exhaled, the corners of his mouth lifting in a sad, rueful smile. "I know. But I needed to see you. To explain. About why I left... why I disappeared like that." His eyes flickered away, heavy with memory, "I wanted to call you, message you a hundred times, but I didn't know what your life had become. I didn't want to drag you back into my mess. But after seeing you at the clinic... I couldn't hold it anymore."

Tanvi kept her gaze on him, confused, uncertain, and wary.

"My father was diagnosed with cancer", he said, his voice barely above a whisper. "It was fast. Aggressive. And, a few months later... he was gone." His eyes gleamed at the corners.

He looked up, searching for hers as if seeking forgiveness, understanding, or simply to be seen. "It was... hard. Harder than I knew how to carry. I had to be there for my family. And I wasn't ready to face the world, let alone you."

The rawness in his voice cut through the years of silence. Tanvi's throat tightened. "I'm sorry, Raghav", she whispered. "I never knew."

For a while, neither of them spoke. The years of absence, the weight of things left unsaid, hung thick around them. And somehow, in those few minutes, the tension of years seemed to settle.

"So how come an embryologist?" Tanvi asked, a small, hesitant smile tugging at her lips. "You hated clinics, remember?"

Raghav chuckled softly, taking a sip of coffee. His eyes went distant. "My sister... she was struggling to conceive. Watching her go through it opened my eyes to a world I'd never considered. The science of beginnings – of fragile, impossible miracles of life. I got obsessed." He smiled faintly. "I went to Oxford for Masters in Clinical Embryology. It was gruelling, but I loved it. Came back, started working here."

Tanvi swallowed hard, an ache settling beneath the admiration. "That's... incredible. I always wondered where you disappeared to."

He shifted in his seat, some of the stiffness leaving his shoulders. "And I heard about your boutique. You built something beautiful, Tanvi. I'm proud of you."

She felt a warmth rise in her chest, soft and unexpected. "It wasn't easy. Some days, I wanted to walk away. But it became my anchor."

The moment stretched. Tanvi found herself searching his face, looking for traces of the boy she once knew beneath the man he had become.

"And what about you?" She asked quietly. "Family? Wife? Kids?"

Raghav's smile faltered. He leaned back, folding his hands on the table. "No wife, no kids. I... haven't been able to settle down. I had a few fleeting relationships, but nothing lasting."

His gaze dropped, shadowed by something deeper. He let out a breath, and when he spoke again, it was a confession. "I kept comparing them to you. The way you laughed. The way you believed in things, even when it was hard. I guess I was waiting for you to come back."

The confession hung between them, raw and vulnerable.

A part of Tanvi clenched. She remembered the way he used to look at her – with longing, with awe – and felt the old flutter of something she thought she'd buried forever. She felt herself drawn in, the same kind of attraction she had felt years back in college.

"It's strange", she murmured, her voice a little unsteady, "how the past can catch up with you when you least expect it."

Raghav's hand moved, a tentative brush of his fingers near hers before retreating. "I don't want to complicate your life. I just... I needed you to know."

Tanvi stared down at her hands, her pulse heavy in her ears. His near-touch had left a warmth behind. "Sometimes, silence hurts more than words", she said quietly.

They sat in quiet, the café sounds fading around them – conversations, the clink of cups, distant laughter – a world away from the fragile space they occupied.

At last, Raghav spoke again, his voice soft. “Whatever comes next – the transfer, everything – I hope you find what you’re looking for, Tanvi. Truly.”

She lifted her gaze, offering him a fragile, half-smile. “Thank you, Raghav. I hope you do too.”

Outside, the sky darkened into twilight, but inside, a fragile truce had been forged – between past and present, between two hearts still aching for peace.

The Lift

By the time they left, the café had thinned out. The evening air was cool. They walked toward the lift in silence.

Raghav pressed the call button. The metallic doors slid open with a soft chime, and they both stepped inside.

The air inside felt heavier, dense with all they hadn’t said and everything they’d barely begun to. Tanvi could feel his nearness – the steady warmth of him, the ghost of his cologne, still achingly familiar.

Neither of them spoke.

But when their eyes met in the mirrored wall, something flickered.

A pull. An ache. A dangerous gravity.

Raghav turned slightly toward her, his gaze open, stormy, his hand hovering near hers again.

"I missed you, Tanvi", he murmured, his voice almost breaking.

Her breath caught. The world seemed to narrow to the shallow space between their lips. Her heart pounded, a painful, unsteady drumbeat. A part of her – one she'd locked away for years – ached to close that distance.

His hand lifted, stopping just short of her cheek, waiting.

And then – ding.

The lift doors slid open.

A nurse stepped in from a side corridor, offering them a polite, distracted smile. "Good evening, Dr Raghav."

Tanvi stepped back, the moment shattering like fragile glass.

Reality surged in – Tarun. The embryo. The life she'd built. The cost of what almost happened.

"I... I should go", she stammered, her voice thick.

Raghav straightened, his vulnerability vanishing beneath the mask of professional calm. "Of course."

They stepped out into the corridor. Neither spoke.

Tanvi could still feel the phantom warmth of his almost-touch, the ache of unfinished things.

Without looking back, she walked away.

The cool air prickled against her skin as she stepped into the parking lot. Her heart was still racing, her lips tingling from a kiss that never happened. She hated how easily one conversation, one look, had undone her.

Sliding into the driver's seat, she closed the door with a soft, final click, muffling the world outside. The silence inside was deafening.

Her phone buzzed.

Tarun: *"Hey love, reached home. Come soon. Love you."*

Guilt and tenderness tangled in her chest. She stared at the screen, the weight of what could've happened pressing down.

Tanvi: "*On my way. Love you too.*"

Her fingers trembled as she set the phone down.

The scent of coffee still lingered on her skin. She rested her head against the steering wheel for a moment, taking a deep breath, the evening's weight pressing down on her. The life she had, the dreams she was fighting for, the man who waited for her at home. And the ghost of a love she still hadn't fully let go.

If only words were enough.

She started the engine, the car headlights cutting through the dusk, and drove away – not toward closure, but toward whatever tomorrow would bring.

The day had drained her.

As night settled over the city, wrapping their home in quiet, Tanvi lay awake, the hum of the air conditioner and the distant city noises filling the silence.

She reached for her phone, more out of habit than hope.

And there it was.

A message from Raghav.

Raghav: "*Tanvi, I owe you an apology for today.... I crossed a line I had no right to. I wasn't prepared to see you again, let alone feel what I did. That was unprofessional and selfish. You deserve peace right now, and I promise I'll keep my distance and stay professional from here on.*

I wish you all the strength for your treatment and whatever lies ahead. You'll be an amazing mother someday – I truly hope you get every bit of happiness you've fought for. Take care."

Tanvi stared at the message, her heart heavy and confused.

She typed, erased, and then finally sent:

"Thank you, Raghav. I wish you well, too."

And with that, she turned her phone face down, the glow of the screen fading into darkness.

Outside, the city carried on. Inside, a woman lay between a past that kept pulling her back and a future she was desperately trying to build.

Chapter – 18
The Fragile Hope

The first pale streaks of morning light crept into the room, spilling over the edge of the curtain. Tanvi lay awake, her body heavy with fatigue and her mind a restless churn of thoughts. The city outside was beginning to stir, but the quiet within their bedroom felt suspended, like the hush before a storm.

She turned on her side, watching Tarun sleep. His face, so familiar, so kind, was softened in repose. There were faint lines at the corners of his eyes, evidence of the years they'd carried together. He had been her anchor, her constant, the only person who knew every fracture within her and still chose to stay.

And yet... her heart had betrayed her.

She closed her eyes, but behind the lids was the flicker of those other eyes – sharp, brown, intense. The memory of Raghav's gaze in the elevator lingered like the last strains of a haunting melody. The proximity, the unspoken pull, the old ache she thought she'd buried deep had cracked open like an old wound.

Her phone lay on the side table, the screen dark. She reached for it instinctively, scrolling through her messages. Nothing new. No unread messages from him. A part of her was relieved. Another part – was ashamedly – disappointed.

She turned back, willing herself to be present in the room, with the man beside her.

A while later, Tarun stirred, his breath catching as he woke.

"Hey", he murmured, rubbing his eyes.

"Did you sleep at all?"

Tanvi shrugged, a faint, crooked smile playing on her lips.

"Bits and pieces."

He sat up, placing a hand on her cheek, his thumb tracing the faint shadows under her eyes.

"You don't have to pretend, you know. I get it", he said softly.

"Today's big."

Tanvi swallowed the lump in her throat, her voice barely a whisper.

"I'm scared, Tarun."

"Me too", he admitted. "But you're the strongest person I know."

It was both comfort and burden, being seen as strong.

He got up and moved to the kitchen, clinking cups and humming an old Kishore Kumar tune. Tanvi listened, the domesticity of it, aching in its ordinariness.

When he returned with tea, they sat together in a silence that wasn't heavy, but familiar. Tarun, in his way, tried to fill the space with gentle, hopeful banter.

"You know, I've been thinking", he grinned, "if it's a boy, we should name him, Simba. Kabir sounds old to me now."

Tanvi laughed – a real, warm laugh that surprised her.

"You're impossible", she said, shaking her head.

"Just trying to get a smile out of you", he winked.

And he had. If only for a moment.

The city was waking up as they drove to the clinic. Shops opening shutters, vendors setting up stalls, people heading to work. Life, relentless in its ordinariness, continued even when your world tilted.

The car ride was quiet, save for the soft hum of old Hindi songs on the radio. Tanvi stared out of the window, watching the buildings blur past.

Tarun reached out, squeezing her hand at a traffic signal.

"Whatever happens... we'll figure it out," he said.

She nodded, but her throat was too tight to speak.

At the Clinic

Inside the clinic, everything was a routine of quiet efficiency. Consent Forms, signatures, measured words from Dr Meera about embryo grade and chances and hope.

"We'll transfer the one euploid one. It looks promising", Dr Meera smiled.

"And then... we wait."

That word again – "wait". Tanvi had spent years waiting. For lines on a stick, for reports, for answers, for hope to mean something.

She was asked to change into the hospital gown and lay on the sterile OT bed as nurses prepped her. The procedure itself was quick, a gentle, precise placement under the ultrasound. The embryo – their fragile hope - PICKLE – was now inside her.

As she moved out of the procedure room to the recovery room, she saw him again.

Raghav, in the light blue scrubs. He appeared from the adjacent lab hallway. Clipboard in hand, face impassive, but his eyes betrayed him. They always did.

Their eyes met – a flicker, a spark, a moment.

A thousand conversations, a thousand regrets compressed into a single glance.

Neither of them spoke.

And that was somehow worse.

Tanvi waited in the recovery room for her prescription and instructions. While she was waiting, her gaze shifted to the pale blue wall opposite her bed. A small framed poem hung there, its delicate cursive lettering set against a faded watercolour background. She squinted, reading it line by line.

Hope

Life isn't easy -
It's a journey of ups and downs,
Of quiet smiles and heavy frowns.
So what if you stumble, or fail,
Each fall teaches you how to sail.

There is no shame in feeling low,
No disgrace in letting emotions show.
So speak your heart- talk or shout,
Sometimes the words can cast the darkness out.

When times are gloomy, when nights feel long,
A conversation can make you strong.
It softens grief eases the strain,
And leaves behind a gentle, tolerable pain.

You need not always be right,
But give yourself the will to fight.
The world may seem to close the doors,
But perhaps you've missed a turn, a path or something more.

This too is a fleeting phase,
A chapter which will be lost in future days.
Till then hold on, and stay strong,
Trust the creator, to whom we all Belong.

And when it feels too heavy to cope.
Remember:
At the end of the tunnel, there is often a ray of Hope.

˜ **Dr Manisha T Kundnani**

The words felt as though they were meant for her, as if some unknown hand had placed them there just for this moment. She felt an unexpected warmth bloom in her chest, a thread of calm tugging at the knots inside her. By the time she reached the last line- "At the end of the tunnel, there's often a ray of hope" – her eyes pricked with tears she hadn't realised she had been holding back.

A nurse walked in quietly with the file and discharge instructions, pausing as she saw Tanvi staring at the frame.

"It's beautiful, isn't it?" the nurse said gently. One of our doctors wrote it- Dr Manisha. She penned it years ago for patients like you, waiting in this very room.

Tanvi swallowed the lump in her throat and nodded.

"Yes, its perfect", she whispered.

Back Home

The rest of the day blurred. Tarun fussed, ordering her favourite soup, settling beside her for a mindless movie she barely registered. He tried his best to distract her. And she tried her best to let him.

When night fell, the house settled into its own quiet rhythm – the hum of the refrigerator, the soft sigh of curtains against the windowpane. Tarun lay beside her, his breathing even, one arm flung carelessly over her waist, anchoring her to this life they'd built.

But Tanvi's eyes remained open, staring into the darkness.

She should have felt peace. She should have felt relieved. The embryo was inside her. The transfer had gone well. The doctors were optimistic. The odds were better this time.

And yet – the storm within her hadn't allayed.

It wasn't just about the embryo, or the silent prayers she whispered into the dark. It was about the things no one could see: the grief she'd tucked away, the fractures in her heart, the old ache of unfinished stories; the magnetic pull of a memory she shouldn't still feel; the bitter guilt of it.

She pressed a hand against her lower abdomen, over the tiny, unseen promise now inside her.

"Please stay", she whispered into the dark. "I don't think I can take another loss."

A tear slipped free, tracing the line of her cheek. She let it fall.

Tomorrow would come with its facades and small talk. Another ordinary day pretending nothing had shifted.

But for tonight, in the fragile, uncertain dark – she allowed herself to hope.

It was reckless. It was necessary.

Because sometimes, hope is all you have.

And right now, it was everything.

Chapter – 19
The Silent Betrayal

The clinic had sent them home with instructions and pamphlets. Tanvi's abdomen was tender, her body heavy with hormones, but it wasn't the physical discomfort that gnawed at her – it was the wait after the embryo transfer, the cruellest kind of limbo.

Two weeks. Fourteen long, aching days before a blood test would confirm or destroy everything.

Each day stretched endlessly, weighed down by expectation and dread. Tanvi followed every instruction to the letter – no caffeine, no strenuous movement, no stress – though stress was the only thing she could feel.

The first few days passed in a fog of enforced optimism. She took a break from work, working from home when she could. No new orders – she'd instructed her staff firmly. She wanted to be cautious, more careful than ever.

Tarun did everything right. He cooked her breakfast, made her laugh with bad romcoms, left little notes and brought her flowers. He tried. God! he tried. But beneath the surface, something had cracked. The unspoken weight of it all was pulling her under, and she was riding a silent roller coaster all by herself.

On the fourth day, a harmless conversation split open the fault line.

"Tanvi, you shouldn't be on your phone so much", Tarun said lightly as she scrolled through an IVF support group thread.

"It's not good for your stress levels."

She looked up, exhaustion bruising her gaze.

"I'm not made of glass, Tarun. And neither is this embryo."

"I didn't mean that..."

"Yes, you did." The words came out sharper than she intended. "You want me to smile, stay positive, act like everything's perfect. It's not perfect. It's terrifying."

Tarun stiffened.

"I'm trying to hold us together, Tanvi. This isn't easy for me either."

A long, brittle silence settled between them.

Tanvi looked away, her chest aching. She wasn't angry at him. Not really. She was angry at the wait, at her body, at the unfairness of it all. But he was the only one standing close enough to bleed on.

Tarun left the room, the door clicking softly shut behind him.

And right then – her phone vibrated.

Raghav: *"I know it's the hardest part now. If you need to talk... I'm around."*

Her fingers hovered over the screen.

She shouldn't reply. She knew it was reckless. Dangerous. But in that fragile, frayed moment, she craved someone who wouldn't tell her to stay positive. Someone who wouldn't look at her like she might shatter.

And Raghav – for all his flaws – saw the storm in her.

Tanvi: *"I can't breathe."*

The reply was instant.

Raghav: *"Come for a drive. No questions. No advice."*

She stared at the message. The apartment felt like a cage. Before logic could intervene, she grabbed her sling bag, slipped into her sandals, and texted Tarun that she was stepping out for some air.

He didn't reply.

And in that cracked, careless moment – she didn't care.

The Mumbai evening pressed heavy and humid, the streets alive with the restless, unrelenting pulse of a city that never paused, not even for heartbreak.

Raghav's car waited a block away. She slid into the passenger seat wordlessly. Neither of them spoke as he drove, aimless, the FM playing forgotten old Hindi tracks. The streetlights flickered past like scattered stars.

It wasn't the kind of silence that needed filling – it was the kind you shared with someone who knew words would only ruin it.

At last, Raghav spoke.

"I'm not asking if you're okay. I know you're not. And that's okay."

Tanvi let out a bitter smile. "Thank you for not pretending."

"You know what I hate most about this? This hope", she whispered. "It doesn't feel like hope anymore. It feels like a threat."

He glanced at her, half-smiling.

"Hope's a cruel thing when it comes with terms and conditions."

She laughed despite herself, a quiet, broken sound. The heaviness between them eased for a heartbeat.

"I remember when my sister had her second failed cycle", Raghav said softly. "Everyone told her to manifest good vibes. To stay positive. She wanted to smash something. I took her to Marine Lines. She screamed at the sea for twenty minutes. Then we ate *sev puri*. It didn't fix anything. But it helped."

"I could use some *sev puri*", Tanvi murmured.

"Deal." He turned the car toward the coast.

They parked by the sea face, the air cooler here, tinged with salt and the scent of the restless city. Waves crashed against ancient rocks, the sound folding around them.

They stood there, side by side, saying nothing.

"I fought with Tarun today", Tanvi admitted at last. "He's trying so hard. And I... I feel like I'm two seconds away from breaking."

Raghav didn't offer advice. He didn't tell her to be strong. He just listened.

"You don't have to carry it all alone", he said quietly. "Not with me. Not here."

The words felt reckless. The moment heavier than it should've been.

Their hands brushed, and this time he didn't let go.

She looked at him – confusion, grief, and a yearning, which she was terrified to name tangled in her chest.

He glanced at her, hesitant.

"I sometimes wonder... if I hadn't left back then – would we have made it?"

Her eyes blurred with unshed tears.

"Don't ask that, Raghav. It's too late for those questions."

But her heart ached – not just for what she'd lost, but for everything she was afraid to want.

Raghav leaned in and kissed her, soft and aching.

"I miss us, Tanvi. I wish I could go back."

She stood there, motionless.

A part of her wanted to pull away. Another part clung to the weightless peace of the moment.

And then – her phone buzzed.

Tarun: "*Come home. I made tea.*"

Reality crashed in.

A home.

An embryo.

A husband waiting.

Tanvi stepped back.

"I should go."

Raghav nodded, something breaking in his gaze.

The drive back was quiet.

"Call me if you want to talk again. I'll always be there for you, Tanvi." His words held longing, a stubborn tenderness.

As she walked away, she felt the burn of his eyes on her back – and a hollow ache throbbed in her chest – not for him, but for the girl she'd been before life forced her to choose.

When she entered the apartment, the lights were low, two mugs of tea on the table. Neither of them spoke. They sipped in silence, the unspoken filling the room like a ghost.

And for the first time in days, something stirred inside Tanvi.

Not perfect. Not safe. But alive.

The days that followed were a blur.

Tarun tried in his way – soups, awkward jokes, notes by the bedside. But the quiet distance between them only stretched wider. Words turned sharp too easily. Apologies felt mechanical.

And in those silent hours, Raghav became something else.

Their messages grew frequent. Not flirtatious – not yet. But intimate in the way that made her stomach twist.

He remembered the little things – her obsession with Nutella toast, her habit of doodling anxious spirals. He asked about the boutique, about a dress she'd once dreamt of designing.

He listened when she whispered her fears which she couldn't voice to Tarun. How she hated her own body for betraying her. How she dreaded the beta hCG result more than anything else.

And Raghav made her feel seen.

One evening, when the cramps worsened and anxiety gnawed at her insides, she called him – without thinking.

"Can you talk?" Her voice cracked.

"I'm at the lab", he said softly. "But for you? Always."

They spoke for over an hour. About embryo grading, about old indie songs, about what made them feel most alive.

And when she finally hung up, something in her chest felt lighter.

And something darker flickered too.

Because somewhere, deep inside, she knew this wasn't harmless. It wasn't physical. Not yet. But it was a kind of betrayal – and in some ways, the most dangerous kind.

That night, as she lay in bed, Tarun's arm draped across her waist, his breathing steady, her phone blinked softly.

Raghav: *"I hope today wasn't too hard. If you need to talk, you know where I am."*

She stared at the message, her chest tightening, guilt and longing warring inside her.

And in those suspended moments she realised the infidelity wasn't just in the kiss. It was in the messages sent at midnight. It was in the choice, in whom you reach for when the world caves in.

It was this – the quiet, invisible thread pulling her somewhere she knew she shouldn't go.

She typed, *"I'm okay. Thank you."*

Paused.

Deleted it.

Her thumb hovered over the screen. She finally placed the phone face-down without replying.

Even with Tarun holding her, she felt lonelier than ever.

The city outside moved in restless waves. Somewhere, a train clattered by. The embryo inside her clung to life, while the life she'd built with Tarun frayed silently at the edges.

And as sleep finally took her, one thought lingered – uninvited, unshakable.

Is this the worst mistake of her life?

Chapter – 20
The Echo of Results

Dawn came quietly, slipping through the sheer curtains of their bedroom like a hesitant guest. The sky was a muted grey-blue, the city's usual chaos still hushed in those fragile, early hours. But inside Tanvi, the storm never rested.

She lay on her side, watching the light shift across the ceiling, her thoughts heavy and unrelenting. Today. Today, by evening, she would know. An embryo inside her body, clinging to hope, or nothing at all.

Her stomach twisted at the thought.

Behind her, Tarun stirred, sensing the unease even in sleep. A moment later, his arm slid around her waist, pulling her back against him.

"You're awake", he murmured, his voice rough with sleep.

"Couldn't sleep", she whispered.

He pressed a kiss into her hair. "Come here."

For the first time in days, she let herself lean into him fully, his steady heartbeat against her back. It wasn't the kind of closeness that fixed things, but it was the kind that reminded her they were still here, still trying.

"I'm sorry", Tarun said softly. "For not... knowing how to be better at this."

Tanvi closed her eyes, the tightness in her chest loosening just a fraction. "It's not your job to fix this, Tarun. It's ours. Together."

She felt him nod. "We've been through worse, haven't we?"

A small, fragile smile tugged at her lips. "Yeah. Remember our first apartment? The one with the leaking ceiling and nosy neighbour?"

Tarun chuckled against her hair. "And the world's tiniest kitchen. We made it work."

They lay like that, the past folding around them like a soft blanket. In that moment, Tanvi felt it – a warmth, a tether, the ache of loving someone not because they made everything better, but because they stayed even when nothing was.

She turned to face him, their foreheads touching. "Thank you... for not giving up on me."

His eyes softened, a flicker of relief breaking through the weariness. "Never, Tanvi."

For a while, they just lay there, not speaking. The city began to wake around them, but inside that room, time slowed. And though the uneasiness of the test lingered, for a fleeting heartbeat, Tanvi remembered why she had chosen this man, this life, these years.

The morning came sharp and unkind.

The clinic's sterile brightness felt harsher than usual. Tanvi sat in the waiting room, fingers clenched around her phone, the blood test requisition crumpled in her lap. Tarun was beside her, his palm covering hers, both of them silent.

Every glance from a nurse felt like a sentence. Every ring of the reception phone a small, cruel reminder that life was carrying on while theirs teetered at a ledge.

The blood draw was quick. A prick, a few exchanged words Tanvi couldn't remember, and then they were outside in the thick, sticky heat of a Mumbai morning.

"Should we grab something to eat?" Tarun asked, his attempt at normalcy sounding a little desperate.

Tanvi shook her head. "Let's just... go home."

Back at home, the hours crawled by. She lay on the couch, mind racing, every twinge in her abdomen a cruel guessing game. Tarun busied himself in the kitchen, overcompensating with sandwiches neither of them ate.

At one point, her phone buzzed.

A message.

Raghav: *"Thinking of you. Wishing you all the luck in the world today, Tanvi. You deserve this."*

Tanvi stared at the screen, her heart tightening in its old, complicated way. It wasn't flirtation. It wasn't even inappropriate. But it was a voice from a part of her heart she wasn't sure how to silence.

She didn't reply.

Instead, she looked up to find Tarun standing in the doorway, watching her.

"Anything important?" He asked.

She hesitated, then shook her head. "Just... a friend."

He nodded, accepting it.

The lie, small as it was, lodged like a pebble in her throat.

Her mind kept wandering- The phone would ring soon. A number would flash on the screen. A voice would speak, and their life would tilt one way or the other.

Tanvi closed her eyes, feeling Tarun's hand slip into hers again.

The hours moved like honey on a cold day.

Slow. Relentless. Sticky.

Tanvi scrolled aimlessly through old photographs on her phone – random sunsets, a stray puppy outside her boutique, the *Karva Chauth* selfie from years ago where her eyes were bright and hope hadn't yet learned how to hurt.

Tarun pretended to work, his laptop open on the dining table, his gaze rarely leaving the screen but his hands barely touching the keyboard.

By afternoon, the house felt heavy, saturated with waiting. Every sound sharpened – the dull hum of the fridge, the whir of the ceiling fan, the occasional horn from the road outside.

And then finally, the phone rang.

Tanvi's heart lurched into her throat.

It was the clinic.

For a second, neither of them moved. The screen blinked with Dr Meera's number. Tarun reached for her hand. She picked up.

"Hello?"

"Tanvi?" It was Dr Meera's calm, practiced voice. "I have your beta hCG result."

Tanvi's stomach clenched. She squeezed Tarun's fingers so hard his knuckles turned white.

"It's... positive, Tanvi."

A beat.

A second one.

Her breath caught.

Positive.

The word hung in the air – fragile, unfamiliar, and holy.

"Your beta HCG is 412", Dr Meera continued gently. "It's a good number for now. We'll need to repeat it in 48 hours to be sure it's rising well."

Tanvi couldn't speak. Couldn't move.

"Tanvi?"

"I – yes. Yes. Thank you, doctor", she managed, her voice a hoarse whisper.

"Please see me tomorrow at the clinic for further instructions", Dr Meera added.

Tanvi ended the call and sat there, the world narrowing to the heartbeat in her ears.

"What is it?" Tarun asked, searching her face.

She looked up at him. And for the first time in what felt like years, her lips curved.

"It's positive."

The words felt strange, like trying out a new language. But the way Tarun's face crumpled – with relief, disbelief, and gratitude – she knew it was real.

And just like that, the dam broke. She dissolved into tears – messy, gasping sobs that tasted like relief, grief, exhaustion. Tarun pulled her into his arms, holding her so tightly she could feel his heartbeat pounding against hers.

They clung to each other, a tangle of limbs and tears and silent promises.

No dramatic declarations. No sweeping music. Just two people, exhausted and a little broken, holding on because that was what they did.

"I told you", he murmured into her hair. "You're stronger than you think."

Tanvi let herself cry into his chest. Cry for the months behind them, for the months ahead, for the little flicker of life growing somewhere deep inside her.

And for the man who had stayed, even when it wasn't easy.

Later that evening, after the calls to her mother and best friend, after Tarun ordering her favourite Chinese takeout and them half-heartedly watching a mindless sitcom, after the first lightness in days – her phone buzzed.

A message.

Raghav: *"Heard the result. Congratulations, Tanvi. I hope you're okay."*

Simple. No overstepping. No implied longing.

But she could almost hear his voice in those words. That steady, familiar calm that had kept her afloat through the worst.

Tanvi stared at the message for a long while, the TV blaring some absurd laugh track in the background, Tarun in the kitchen fixing them tea.

But in that moment, she didn't reply.

Not because she didn't care. Not because it didn't matter.

But because, for this moment in this fragile, golden sliver of time – she wanted to be fully here. With the man she had chosen, in the life they had rebuilt one shattered piece at a time.

She placed the phone facedown, the message unread.

And when Tarun came back and passed her a mug, their fingers brushed – and something unspoken passed between them.

Not perfect. Not healed. But alive. Together.

For now.

For now, the peace lingered – fragile and fleeting.

Chapter – 21
The Storm Within, The Ruins Outside

Tarun slept peacefully beside her, but Tanvi lay awake, eyes tracing the cracks in the ceiling she'd memorized a hundred sleepless nights before.

This had become her routine.

And yet tonight was meant to be different. Happy. Peaceful. She should have felt safe, anchored by the tiny spark of life growing inside her. But instead, she was restless – her mind battling itself in a quiet, relentless war.

The messages from Raghav, which had felt like a lifeline these past few weeks, now terrified her. They weren't harmless. They weren't innocent. They were dangerous.

Where am I heading with this?

She didn't know how it had come to this. How a face from a lifetime ago could still carry the power to unravel her so completely. How one message had turned into a hundred. She'd thought she'd buried that chapter of her past so deep, it would never claw its way back. But ghosts have a way of lingering – in old photographs, in the sterile scent of hospital corridors, in names whispered when no one else is listening.

She should have walked away the moment she saw him.

She should have.

But there had been something – not in him, but in herself – flicker of the girl she once was – the one who laughed without counting the consequences, who believed in love without conditions, in beginnings without endings. And in those moments, when Tarun was trying to be brave for both of them, when the weight of hope and fear threatened to crush her, it was Raghav who reminded her of the version of herself before life carved away at her edges.

And maybe that's what she was chasing.

Not him.

Her.

The girl who wasn't defined by medical reports, waiting rooms, or whispered reassurances. The one who believed in wild, reckless beginnings.

But whatever this was – this fragile thread she'd been holding on to – it was dangerous now. It wasn't just about her anymore. There was a child. Or the fragile hope of one.

And Tarun. God! Tarun.

He didn't deserve this. He deserved a wife who chose him every single day. Not one caught between the ghosts of her past and the life she promised him. Every time she let a message from Raghav linger, every time her heart skipped at the sight of his name on her screen, she wasn't just betraying her marriage. She was betraying herself.

Because inside her, the truth was clear – *she didn't love Raghav.*

Not anymore.

She loved the memory of what they were. The way he reminded her of a time before life cracked her open. But you can't build a future on nostalgia. You can't build a home on quicksand.

And now, it was time to stop.

For Tarun.

For the child she ached to bring into the world.

For herself.

It wouldn't be easy. Endings never are. But some ghosts need to be laid to rest so the living can breathe.

She picked up her phone, her fingers trembling slightly as she typed.

"Can we meet tomorrow? Café across the clinic. 4 PM, after my appointment."

His reply came almost instantly.

"Yes, definitely. We should celebrate the result."

She didn't answer.

Instead, she placed the phone face down on the bedside table, turned toward Tarun, and let his hand find hers. The ache inside her softened, but sleep stayed elusive.

Storms don't sleep.

They wait.

And tomorrow, she would finally face hers.

The Cafe

The café was half-empty, the late afternoon sun slanting in through the glass. The hum of conversation and the clatter of cups felt distant, like a world she no longer belonged to.

Tanvi sat at a corner table, facing the window, watching people pass by.

She heard him before she saw him. The familiar gait, the soft scrape of a chair being pulled out. And then Raghav was there, sitting across from her, a hesitant smile tugging at the corner of his mouth.

"You look... different", he said softly, as if afraid of breaking the fragile air between them.

"I am", Tanvi replied, her voice steady despite the storm inside her.

For a moment, neither spoke. The waitress came and went. Two cups of coffee appeared. Neither of them touched those.

Tanvi finally broke the silence, "This needs to stop, Raghav, the messages, these meetings, we can't go on like this."

Tanvi looked up and her eyes met Raghav's. The same eyes that once felt like home, now heavy with things unspoken.

"I came to say goodbye."

He blinked, a flicker of hurt crossing his face before he masked it with a small, sad smile. "I figured."

"Raghav... these past weeks... I let something happen that shouldn't have. I told myself it was harmless.

That it was old friends reconnecting. But it wasn't that." Her voice cracked, and she hated herself for it.

He shook his head.

"I thought I was chasing you," she continued, her eyes stinging, "but I was chasing the girl I used to be when you knew me. Before infertility clinics. Before the ache of empty rooms and negative reports. Before the nights I cried myself to sleep without letting Tarun hear me. I was chasing her. Not you."

Raghav was silent, his gaze dropping to the table.

"And I realized", she whispered, "I can't bring her back. She's gone. And maybe that's okay. Maybe I don't need to resurrect her. I need to become someone new. For Tarun. For the child I'm trying to carry. For myself."

"Tanvi..." he began, but she lifted her hand, stopping him.

"I don't love you anymore, Raghav. I love the memory of us. And I think you know that too."

He let out a breath, a mixture of relief and heartbreak. "Yeah", he said hoarsely. "I know."

"I need to close this chapter. No more messages. No more quiet meetings. No more ghosts."

Tears clung to her lashes, but she blinked them away. She wouldn't break now.

"I wish you peace and happiness, Raghav. I truly do. I wish you find your love too. But you can't be a part of my story anymore."

A long, aching silence stretched between them.

Raghav finally stood up. "I'm sorry," he said softly, his voice breaking. "For everything. For leaving back then. For being here now. You deserved more."

Tanvi managed a small, bittersweet smile. "So do you."

He hesitated, as if wanting to say something else, then thought better of it. He turned and walked out.

Tanvi sat there, alone at the table, the untouched coffee cooling between her hands.

And for the first time in months, the storm inside her quieted.

The ache didn't leave. The grief didn't vanish. But it felt... lighter.

A beginning, stitched from endings.

She took out her phone, opened Tarun's message from earlier: *"Hope all went ok with the doctor. I am home early, come soon. Waiting. Love."*

Her heart fluttered; it was for the right reasons this time.

She typed back: *"Yeah, all well. Love you."*

The storm had passed. At least for now. And whatever came next, she was ready.

The house was bathed in the soft glow of evening when Tanvi returned. The living room lights were dim, and the faint hum of an old Bollywood song playing somewhere in the background. The scent of ginger and cardamom hung in the air.

Tarun was in the kitchen, his back to her, stirring something on the stove. He wore one of his faded college T-shirts, the one with a tiny hole near the hem she always teased him about.

For a moment, Tanvi stood by the door, watching him – this man who had, without theatrics or grand declarations, built a life around her; who had stayed when the hope thinned; who had held her when she broke down.

"Hey", she said softly.

He turned, a boyish grin spreading across his face. "There she is. I was about to call you."

She stepped closer, slipping her arms around his waist, resting her cheek against his back. It wasn't dramatic. It wasn't cinematic. It was ordinary in a way that felt extraordinary tonight.

"I'm sorry I've been... distant", she murmured.

He stilled for a moment, then turned in her arms, cupping her face in his hands. His thumbs brushed the remnants of unshed tears from beneath her eyes.

“I know”, he said gently. “I’ve been scared too, Tanvi. Scared of what the reports would say, of what it’s been doing to you. I didn’t know how to fix it. I still don’t. But I never stopped being here.”

A tear slipped down her cheek. Not from grief, but from relief.

“I don’t deserve you, you know.” She wanted to confess, tell him the truth, but she was scared of the consequences – of what it might do to their relation.

“Maybe not,” he teased, a small, crooked smile breaking through. “But you’re stuck with me.”

They stood like that in the middle of their tiny kitchen, arms around each other, the storm of the past weeks finally beginning to settle.

The pressure cooker whistled in the background.

They sat down to dinner, not as a couple untouched by pain, but as two people learning how to hold on to each other through it.

And when Tarun reached across the table to hold her hand, Tanvi realized – this was what staying looked like. Not perfect. Not effortless. But real.

Later that night, the house settled into stillness. The faint glow of streetlights slipped in through the window blinds, drawing soft lines across the walls.

Tanvi changed into her old cotton nightshirt, the one with a worn-out print, and slipped under the covers. Tarun was already there, scrolling aimlessly through his phone, the blue light reflecting off his face.

For a while, neither spoke. The silence wasn't tense – it was the kind that wrapped around them like an old, familiar quilt.

Tanvi turned to her side, watching him in the dim light.

"You okay?" He asked, sensing her gaze.

She hesitated, then nodded. "Yeah... I am."

He leaned in, kissed her forehead – a quiet, anchoring thing – and switched off the bedside lamp.

In the darkness, Tanvi moved closer, resting her head against his chest. His arms closed around her without hesitation.

She didn't tell him about Raghav. Not tonight.

Some truths could wait.

Some closures had to be private.

And some love – like Tarun's – was steady enough to hold her through both.

As sleep claimed them, Tanvi felt, for the first time in weeks, that she might just be okay. That whatever shadows lingered, the light hadn't left entirely.

Not yet.

Not while he was here. He was her safe space. And will be forever.

Chapter – 22
A Name He Shouldn't Have Seen

The house was unusually quiet that evening. A gentle drizzle tapped against the windowpanes, the kind of rain that made the city smell of wet earth and old secrets.

Tanvi was in the shower. Tarun sat on the couch, flipping through a cricket highlights reel he wasn't really watching.

Her phone, left carelessly on the coffee table, buzzed.

He glanced at it instinctively. The screen lit up.

Raghav: *"I'm sorry for what happened between us. I wish things were different. I wish you all the happiness always. Take care of yourself, Tanvi."*

The world seemed to narrow in that instant.

Tarun's hand, mid-motion to pick up his cup of tea, froze. The air around him thickened. A distant commentary voice from the TV faded into a hollow echo.

"What happened between us"

And his wife's name – *Tanvi* – at the end of it like a cruel punctuation mark.

A cold, prickling sensation crept up his spine.

The bathroom door clicked open. Tanvi stepped out in a towel, drying her hair, unaware.

But something in the room had shifted.

She caught his expression immediately – a mixture of confusion, disbelief, and a pain so raw it made her chest constrict.

"What... what happened?" She asked, her voice a notch too high.

Tarun held up the phone wordlessly, the message still glowing against the dim light of the room.

"Who's Raghav?" His voice wasn't raised. It was worse – steady. Controlled. The kind of calm before a storm.

Tanvi's world tilted.

"I... It's not what you think."

"Then you better start explaining what it is."

Her throat felt like sandpaper. The room, the rain, the hum of the ceiling fan – everything blurred.

"He's... someone from before. Before you."

"And you've been... talking?"

She nodded, swallowing hard. "It wasn't like that, Tarun. I swear. It was... complicated. I needed to end it. I met him once. For closure."

Tarun let out a brittle, humourless laugh. "Closure? Tanvi – you're carrying our child, we're fighting every damn day to hold on to this life, and you're messaging some old lover?"

"I wasn't trying to hurt you", she whispered.

"But you did."

His words landed like stones in the pit of her stomach.

"I didn't tell you because I was ashamed. Because it was stupid, and reckless, and it didn't mean what you think it did. I just... I was scared. I needed to remember who I was before everything turned into hospitals and injections and reports. And he was a stupid, fleeting reminder of that."

"And what about me, Tanvi?" Tarun's voice cracked. "What am I? Just the guy holding your hand while you mourn someone else?"

Tears streamed down her face. "No! God, no! It was never about him. It was about me trying not to drown."

The rain outside turned heavier, each drop slamming against the glass like a drumbeat.

For a long, unbearable minute, they stood in the same room, but miles apart.

Finally, Tarun exhaled, every ounce of fight draining out of him. "I need some air", he said, grabbing his keys.

"Tarun, please–"

But he was already at the door.

It closed with a soft click.

And the only sound left in the room was the rain, and Tanvi's sobs.

The night passed, and morning light crept in. Tanvi hadn't slept. Not really. She'd drifted in and out, waking at every sound, imagining the soft jingle of Tarun's keys or his footsteps outside. But the door never opened.

He hadn't come back.

Not until dawn.

She heard the lock click faintly around five. The soft shuffle of shoes being kicked off. Then silence.

She didn't get up. She didn't know how to.

It was almost seven when she found him sitting at the dining table, staring into a cup of untouched tea. His eyes were bloodshot, his hair a mess, dark circles bruising the skin beneath his eyes. But it wasn't the fatigue that gutted her – it was the quiet defeat in his posture.

She took a deep breath, holding her mug like a shield.

"I need to tell you everything," she said, her voice hoarse.

Tarun didn't look up. "Do you?"

"Yes. Because... you deserve that. Because I can't live with half-truths anymore."

He let out a slow, exhausted sigh. "Go ahead."

And so, she told him.

About Raghav. About college.

About the party where they met.

How it had been wild, messy, intoxicating – the kind of love you only fall into when you're twenty and think the world bends to your will.

She told him about the months they spent tangled in each other's lives. About how Raghav had this way of making her feel seen, alive, and reckless. How it spiralled, how they clung to each other.

And the night when she found out she was pregnant.

Tarun's head jerked up at that, his eyes narrowing. But he didn't interrupt.

"I was barely twenty-two", she whispered, tears slipping freely now. "I was terrified. It was a mistake, I don't even remember anymore. It was a disaster. We fought. I was scared out of my mind. My parents would've disowned me. I… I terminated it."

Her voice cracked.

"I left that life. I buried it so deep because it hurt so much, Tarun. And I promised myself I'd never look back."

She wiped her face with trembling fingers.

"And then when we walked into that clinic… and he was there. I didn't know how to handle it. I didn't plan it. I didn't seek him out. It was like this… ghost, crashing back into a life I'd rebuilt. And I was angry, and terrified, and curious. Not about him – about me. About the girl I used to be. And for a few stupid days, those messages made me feel like I wasn't this broken, desperate woman chasing a miracle that kept slipping through our fingers."

Tarun stared at her. His face was unreadable. His silence was worse than shouting.

"I'm sorry," she whispered. "Not for what happened back then. But for what I did to us now. For not telling you when I should have. For letting it get this far."

The clock on the wall ticked too loudly.

Finally, Tarun spoke. His voice was low, but steady.

"I don't even know what hurts more right now. That you lied to me... or that for all these months, while I was losing sleep over you, over us, over every injection, every failed report, you had this... escape. This other world I wasn't part of."

"It wasn't a world", she whispered. "It was a mistake. A weak, stupid mistake."

He pushed back his chair and stood. Walked to the window, staring out at the rain-soaked city.

"I don't know what to do with this, Tanvi" he said softly. "I don't know how to look at you and not see him."

Tears blurred her vision. "Then see me" she begged. "See me now. The woman who stayed. Who fought beside you. Who made mistakes but never stopped loving you. Who wants this life with you, Tarun."

A long silence.

Then, without turning, he spoke.

"I need time."

She closed her eyes, her heart breaking open, because she knew –

Love didn't erase everything. It stitched over wounds, but the scars stayed. And now it would be a long, brutal wait to see if theirs would heal, or finally split for good.

Chapter – 23
The Heartbeat Between Us

The days after that morning blurred into one another like smudged watercolours on a damp page.

Tanvi and Tarun moved around each other like polite strangers inhabiting the same space. Words became practical necessities – "Have you eaten?" "Your prescription is on the table", "I'll be late." The distance between them wasn't loud. It was a quiet, relentless ache. The absence of things once taken for granted.

No lingering good mornings.

No teasing remarks.

No stolen, wordless moments where eyes met and said everything.

Tanvi found herself throwing hours into work, sketching designs she didn't even like. Anything to keep her hands moving, her mind distracted. Because when the boutique lights dimmed and she lay alone on her side of the bed, the guilt came for her like a tide she couldn't outrun.

Tarun did the same. Early mornings, late nights. Coffee cups stacking up on his desk at the office, unopened messages from friends, calls to his mother returned with a half-hearted "I'm busy."

One night, Tarun sat alone in the dimly lit living room, the hum of the refrigerator and the ticking clock the only company in the house. Tanvi's side of the bed had been cold for days, though she still slept in it.

He scrolled aimlessly through his phone, pausing at an old photograph of them at a friend's wedding. Tanvi's face was caught mid-laugh, a curl of hair falling across her cheek, and he remembered how fiercely he'd loved that girl – reckless, radiant, his. The kind of love that felt bulletproof once.

Now, a chasm stretched between them, built of unspoken words and silent betrayals. Of grief neither of them knew how to name. The woman who lay beside him each night wasn't the girl in that photograph, and maybe he wasn't the same man either.

His thumb brushed over the screen, as if he could trace the memory of her. He thought of the nights when she would hum old Hindi songs in the kitchen while making ginger tea, insisting that the secret to happiness was extra grated ginger and a pinch of cardamom. It wasn't much, but it had felt like home. He couldn't remember the last time their home had smelled of cardamom.

Tarun clenched his jaw, his throat tightening. He'd always believed that love could endure anything. Illness. Infertility. Even failure. But no one prepared him for the loneliness of loving someone who was slipping away, for the helplessness of watching the person you knew become a stranger you still ached for.

He set the phone down and let the tears come – not loud, not dramatic, but in quiet, stubborn streaks that left salt on his lips.

And in that hollow, aching quiet, a single thought circled in his mind: "*I don't know how to go back to the old times of togetherness*".

He wanted to get up, to walk into their room, to hold her like he used to. To bury his face in her hair and tell her he missed her, even when she was right there. But the brittle truth of betrayal, and the heavy, unyielding weight of his own ego, held him back.

So, he stayed where he was. And the silence pressed in, thick and unforgiving.

Neither of them knew how to reach for the other without reopening old wounds.

And then – it happened.

A single moment. A single shockwave to crack the frozen surface of their grief.

Tanvi was sorting fabric swatches late in the evening when it started. A cramp, sharper than usual, low in her abdomen. She pressed a hand to her stomach, dismissing it. Stress, maybe. She hadn't eaten properly all day.

But then she felt the warmth.

Looked down.

And the blood was there.

A deep, accusing red staining the soft pink of her dress.

For a moment, the room spun. The air seemed to drain from her lungs. She clutched at the table for balance, a sharp gasp escaping her lips.

Her phone shook in her hand as she dialled Tarun's number.

"Bleeding. Please come."

Within minutes, Tarun was at the boutique – breathless, wild-eyed, panic written in every sharp line of his face. Without a word, he swept her into his arms, cursing the traffic, the distance, the delay.

He tried calling Dr Meera, but her phone was not reachable.

The car ride to the hospital was silent except for Tanvi's uneven breathing and the desperate, whispered reassurances from Tarun.

"You'll be fine. The baby will be fine. We'll be fine."

But even he didn't sound convinced.

At the hospital, white coats moved around them like blurs. A drip was inserted into her arm. Injections. Monitors. Blood samples. Questions. The word "threatened abortion" was murmured. "Please inform Dr Meera", one of the nurses said. Tanvi felt like someone had knocked the air from her chest.

No. No, not now. Not after everything.

Tarun paced the waiting area, his hands knotted into fists, his face pale and drawn. Every time a nurse walked by, his eyes darted up, searching for something – anything – that would tell him his world wasn't about to collapse.

Dr Meera came about 30-35 minutes later. Tanvi was shifted to the ultrasound room.

In the ultrasound room, the gel was cold, and the room dim. Tanvi gripped the sheets tightly, her heart pounding so loud she thought it might drown out the machine.

And then – there it was.

A flicker.

Small, stubborn, defiant.

A heartbeat.

Faint but present. Like a tiny drum in the middle of a storm.

"Baby looks fine, I can see the heart beat", Dr Meera remarked, her words reassuring. Tanvi burst into tears – helpless, raw sobs that shook her. Tarun, standing behind her, placed a trembling hand on her shoulder, then her hair, then her cheek.

He pressed his lips to her temple.

"It's okay", he whispered, voice cracking. "We've got this."

Neither knew how long they stayed like that.

Later, in the hospital room, Tanvi lay on the bed, an IV line in her hand. The world outside the window was dusky grey, the city lights beginning to blink awake. Tarun sat beside her, their fingers tentatively intertwined.

It felt fragile, but it felt real.

"I'm sorry", she whispered, tears slipping down the side of her face.

He shook his head. "Don't. Not now. It doesn't matter."

"It does", she insisted. "I was so lost... I made mistakes... I hurt you."

Tarun looked at her, really looked – at the woman he had loved since so many years, who had weathered so much alongside him. And in that moment, all the anger, the hurt, the betrayal shrank beneath the enormity of what they'd almost lost.

He cupped her face. "We almost lost everything today. And none of it – none of it matters more than this. Than you. Than us. Than this little heartbeat."

Tanvi reached for his hand, guiding it to rest over her stomach. His touch was tentative, reverent.

"Let's stop punishing ourselves", she whispered. "Let's stop looking back."

Tarun leaned forward, pressing his forehead to hers.

"We move forward", he murmured. "Whatever comes next – together."

The rain began against the windowpane.

A quiet, steady rhythm.

Much like the tiny heartbeat now safely fluttering within her.

And for the first time in weeks, Tanvi allowed herself to believe they might be okay.

The world outside kept raining, but inside that small hospital room, a heartbeat louder than the storm told them they still had something worth saving.

They left the hospital with bandaged hearts, and promises unspoken. No more ghosts, no more silences. Only what came next.

Some storms don't pass. You just learn to dance in the rain, and cradle what you still have left.

Chapter – 24
Echoes and The New Beginnings

One Year Later

The nursery was a sanctuary.

Soft light filtered through lemon-tinted curtains, painting golden patches on the hardwood floor. The walls, once bare, were now adorned with watercolour animals and soft-hued frames holding memories of a life Tanvi hadn't thought she'd have. The cradle sat by the window – ivory white with a mobile of stars and clouds, swaying gently with the breeze.

Inside, nestled between fleece and lace, lay a tiny bundle of miracles.

A daughter. Their daughter - 'Anvi'.

Tanvi stood beside the crib, fingers trailing the delicate curve of the baby's cheek, where a tuft of inky black hair peeked out from under a woollen cap. She still couldn't believe it sometimes – that this little life had chosen her. Chosen them.

A year ago, she had been a storm of doubt and damage. And now, this.

"Still watching her like you don't believe it's real?" Tarun's voice was soft behind her, teasing, a hand brushing her shoulder.

She turned, a smile tugging at her lips. "I don't think I'll ever stop."

He handed her a cup of coffee, their fingertips grazing. The weight of so much unsaid lingered in the air, but it wasn't heavy anymore. It was just there – part of them, like old scars on skin you'd stopped hiding.

Tarun leaned against the window frame, gazing down at their sleeping daughter.

"She has your hair", he murmured. "And your stubbornness, I'm sure."

Tanvi laughed, leaning into his warmth. "God help us."

In that quiet moment, the past felt like a story from someone else's life. The ghosts had grown quieter. The wounds had scabbed. And what remained was this – a calm, not because everything was flawless, but because they had learned how to be broken together.

Life had crept back in – gently. The boutique was a riot of colours and fabrics.

The chaos of the wedding season was in full swing again – chasing deadlines, swatches scattered like confetti, and music playing low in the background. Tanvi moved through it all with a steadiness she'd reclaimed. Anisha flitted in and out of the office, bridal glow undeniable.

"I still can't believe you're getting married next week", Tanvi teased as Anisha sorted invoices.

Anisha grinned. "Believe it. And I'll finally get to sleep in on weekends without bridezillas calling me at dawn."

Tanvi mock-gasped. "You'll miss this madness."

"I'll miss you more."

They hugged, longer than either expected. There had been a time – not long ago – when even these simple things felt out of reach.

Anisha pulled back, wiping a playful tear. "You'll need a new assistant soon, boss lady."

Tanvi shrugged. "We'll see who fate sends my way."

Fate, it seemed, was already waiting.

The internship interviews were squeezed in between appointments.

A dozen fresh faces. Nervous energy. Shaking hands and hopeful portfolios.

Tanvi flipped through the last resume absently until her gaze landed on a name.

"Raghav Kapoor"

The world stilled for a breath. Her heart gave a small, ridiculous stutter. The inked letters swam before her eyes.

It wasn't him. Of course, it wasn't.

She'd heard from a mutual friend that Raghav had shifted to Bangalore for a new position. It was a passing mention during a casual conversation, the kind of information that once would have snagged at her heart. Now, it barely stirred a ripple.

But names had a way of remembering.

She inhaled, exhaled, placed the resume aside.

A tall, slightly awkward young man with messy hair and an eager grin walked in. He couldn't have been more than twenty-two.

"Hi, ma'am. I'm Raghav Kapoor. Huge fan of your designs. It'd be an honour to learn here."

Tanvi smiled. And not the brittle, practiced kind. A real one. The kind that felt like reclaiming something.

"Welcome, Raghav", she said. "Let's see what you've got."

And in that simple moment, Tanvi realised-

The name wasn't the ghost.

Her past wasn't a prison.

And she wasn't the same woman who stood in the hospital corridor months ago, torn between memory and promise.

She was someone new.

A mother, a survivor, a builder of her own future.

Behind her, Tarun appeared at the doorway, watching.

When the boy left, Tarun crossed the room.

"You okay?"

Tanvi leaned against his chest. "Yes, I'm okay."

And she meant it.

Outside, the cradle shifted as the baby stirred. A soft gurgling sound. A tiny hand curled into a fist.

Life, in all its imperfect, relentless, beautiful way, was moving forward.

And so would she.

Some names stay. Some wounds fade.

Some ghosts leave by storm. Some by silence.

And some – you learn to live alongside, like old songs you no longer listen to, but somehow, still remember the words of.

But Love – the real kind – is the one you choose. The one you fight for when the storm passes.

And for Tanvi, it was finally here.

Not perfect.

But hers.

Author's note

Dear Reader,

If you've made it this far, thank you for walking alongside me through this story.

Pins, Pains & Promises was born from a quiet, persistent ache – one I've witnessed too often in my years as an infertility specialist. Behind every scan, every blood test, every anxious waiting room silence, there are stories like Tanvi and Tarun's. Stories of hope and heartbreak, of unspoken grief and the fragile, stubborn courage it takes to try again.

This isn't a perfect story. It's messy, flawed, and deeply human. Because in real life, the people we love the most are sometimes the ones we hurt the most. And healing rarely comes in grand, cinematic moments. It arrives in the quiet: a trembling hand held in silence, a flicker of life on an ultrasound screen, a promise – made not of certainty, but of effort.

As a doctor, I've seen how infertility tests not just bodies, but relationships, faith, and self-worth. Life doesn't promise us neat, tidy endings. It offers us mornings after sleepless nights, and a chance to keep going.

If you've ever carried an ache, a ghost of what could have been, or loved someone through the storm of it – may you find your own cradle by the window.

And if this story found echoes in your heart, please know this: you are not alone.

With warmth,

Dr Manisha T Kundnani
Infertility Specialist & Author